AWAY FROM KEYBOARD COLLECTION

HIS CODE

PATRICIA D. EDDY

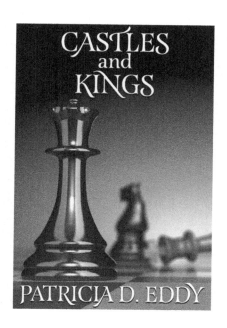

If you love sexy romantic suspense, I'd love to send you a short story set in Dublin, Ireland. Castles & Kings isn't available anywhere except for readers who sign up for my mailing list! Sign up for my newsletter on my website and tell me where to send your free book!
http://patriciadeddy.com.

CAM

"Come on, you sexy thing. Show me what you've got." With a click of the mouse, I compile one of Oversight's modules—the security software package I've spent the past year developing has twenty of the damn things—and sit back to admire my handiwork. On my second screen, a dark square sputters to life, showing me a live video feed of the office and the back of my head. Damn. The messy bun I thought looked so good when I left my condo this morning now has more in common with a rat's nest than anything else. "Show me the still images," I murmur as I tap the keyboard. The screen flickers, and I'm treated to a view of the front lobby, then the parking lot. "Gotcha."

This module's given me fits for a week, and I pump my fist after I shut Oversight down. The office starts to sputter to life, so I grab my cane and head for the coffee machine. I don't know why I drink this over-roasted, bitter brew, but I was up most of the night, courtesy of my lousy hip, and I'm hurting.

Once I've added enough cream to turn the liquid muddy, I take a tentative sip. *Bleck*. But I'm desperate.

"Save some for the rest of us," Lucas calls as he ambles up to the coffee cart.

"I don't know how you drink this swill every day." I dangle his favorite mug in front of him, the one with "Have you tried turning it off and on again?" printed in a pixelated font.

Six-foot-three with dreads that brush his shoulders, Lucas looks more like the next GQ cover model than a badass programmer. He chuckles and dumps approximately half the sugar container into his cup. "Any plans for the weekend?"

"The usual: work, VetNet, Halo. When are you going to join me?"

"When I won't feel bad about beating your ass?"

"I'll have you know I'm undefeated." I jab his shoulder, and he chuckles.

"It'll take more than a single punch to take down my squad. Once this job's done, you and me, ace." He winks. "We'll see who comes out on top."

"Name the time." I arch my brows in challenge, but before Lucas can reply, his phone beeps from inside his jacket. Coffee sloshes over the rim of his mug as he tries to extricate his phone, and I reach for a stack of napkins.

"Shit," Lucas mutters once he's glanced at the screen. Looking vaguely ill, he sets his mug down. "Any chance I can bail a little after three today? I can come in tomorrow to make up the time."

"Hot date?" He doesn't respond, so I shift my gaze from the assignment log scrawled on the office whiteboard to his face. "Must be if you're clamming up over it. Spill."

"I don't know yet." His tone says casual, but there's something deeper behind his eyes. "Could be nothing. You know how it is."

"Luc, I haven't had a relationship in three years. For all I know, the entire dating scene's changed. Do people still do the whole 'getting to know you' bit? Or have we replaced that with stalking someone on social media?" Chuckling, I wait for his response, but when he can only press his lips together, I sober. "Don't mind me." With a gentle pat on his arm, I try to extract my well-worn boot

2

from my mouth. "We're ahead of schedule thanks to your kickass debugging. I want you to be happy. You deserve a break. I hope he's wonderful and you don't come in tomorrow because you're still with him."

His smile flashes briefly before we both amble towards our desks. "Thanks, Cam. I'll make it up to you. Promise."

THE COANA HOTEL glitters in the mid-morning sun—twenty stories of sleek glass and metal capped with a rooftop atrium that offers a view all the way to Mount Rainier.

Royce is late. His terse text message advised me to start without him, and when I protested, he didn't respond. Whatever. I know what needs to be done, and I can meet with LaCosta alone. He's rumored to be a staunch conservative, both in his politics and his social views, but I clean up well enough, and my black blazer hides the tats decorating my arms.

Inside the lobby, the scent of freesia envelopes me, and plush carpet muffles my footfalls. The concierge directs me to the fifth floor, where the rich amber walls and ornate sconces lend the hotel an old-world luxury, even though construction was completed only five years ago.

"Camilla Delgado from Emerald City Security to see Mr. LaCosta," I say when Phillip's pretty blonde assistant greets me.

"Is Mr. Nadiri joining you?" She glances at her computer screen, then back at me, and I try not to squirm as I practice my lie.

"He's been unavoidably detained. Traffic accident in Bellevue." I color my bullshit with a bright smile, though inwardly, I want to throttle Royce. While the actual installation and configuration are all on me, he's supposed to handle the schmoozing.

My phone buzzes—finally. Royce better be downstairs. A quick glance at the screen both irks me and brings a small smile. Royce is still avoiding me, but West—the former SEAL I've gamed with almost every night online—can always raise my spirits.

Halo tonight?

The week's worn me out, and I've skipped my evening gaming sessions. I rush to reply as Phillip's assistant gathers a small stack of files from her desk.

I hope so. Get ready to have your ass kicked.

"Right this way, Ms. Delgado." His assistant opens the inner office door, and when I step inside, Phillip LaCosta rises to offer a firm handshake. With the formalities out of the way, I sit and fold my hands over the pewter handle of my cane, using the familiarity of the ridges and groves to calm my nerves.

"I'm sorry Royce couldn't make it this morning. There was an accident on the bridge from Bellevue." There's always an accident on the bridge. Well, almost always. I hope Phillip doesn't pay attention to traffic reports.

His smile highlights the lines around his mouth. Phillip is pushing seventy, from what I've read, but he appears much younger. "The absurdity of this city's traffic causes no end of problems, doesn't it?"

"It does." *Shit.*

I worry he's going to call me on my lie, but instead, he sighs and leans back in his chair. "Ironically, that's the reason I've asked you here. I'm throwing a party over Labor Day weekend. My daughter is kicking off her campaign for the Senate. Media coverage will be high, and we'll have several members of the City Council present, as well as colleagues from her law firm and four former state representatives. Emma wanted the party at Coana East in Bellevue, but the Department of Transportation decided that's the perfect weekend to tear down the overpass two blocks away. I'd like folks to show up—not be stuck in a traffic nightmare for hours."

I nod, unsure of what this has to do with me, but then he leans forward and with an earnest gaze asks, "Is there any possible way we can bump up the install date for Oversight so it's ready for the party?" He flips through a few pages of his desktop calendar. "Say in…three weeks?

4

I'd push back, but we've never had a contract this big. We're close. If Lucas and I work the weekends...

"I'll compensate your firm for any overtime," Phillip offers as I ponder the ramifications.

Royce's impassioned speech to the office when we took this contract replays in my head. Our big break. Our chance to put our small firm on the map. If I say no, I'll let everyone down. With a deep breath, I force a smile. "We'll make it happen."

Oversight is solid. Wiring the entire hotel in three weeks worries me, but Royce has installers on call. We can do this.

"Fantastic."

SPARKS OF PAIN race up my left thigh, settling into my hip where I'm pretty sure someone's driving a dagger directly into my pelvis. All afternoon, I kept myself going with thoughts of pizza and hard cider, then some *Halo* after the worst of the strain fades. Vicodin goes so well with pepperoni, after all.

Once I've placed the order, I sink into my recliner and open my laptop. You'd think after spending my days programming security software, I'd find something else to do at night, but the men and women I talk to online are my friends. I'm more comfortable behind a keyboard than anywhere else.

Logging onto VetNet, I post a quick greeting: *Been a long day. Everything hurts, and I'm trying to hold off taking a pain pill for a while. Distract me, please.*

As I poke around the various threads, my messenger dings.

WestWind: *You want distraction? I just picked up* Gears of War. *Come join me.*

West, the retired SEAL I've spent most of my nights with—online—ends his message with a YouTube link, and, seconds later, I'm laughing so hard my sides hurt. The puppy on the screen tries to navigate stairs for the first time, and the little yips and squeals as he gives up and runs down the stairs like some Evil-Knievel-

5

wannabe ease the knots in my shoulders and back. My shoulders quake as I type my response.

FlashPoint: *As soon as my pizza shows up. Give me an hour, and I'm all yours.*

WestWind: *All? Don't tease me.*

I choke on my blackberry cider, sending liquid burning down my throat. When I can breathe again, I pause with my fingers on the keyboard. How in the world am I supposed to respond to that? We're...friends. Sort of. Gaming buddies. Though lately, something's shifted in his tone, and my cheeks burn as I realize he's been *flirting*. What's worse, I've flirted back.

What the hell do I do now? In the end, cowardice wins, and I find a clip of baby sloths swaddled in fuzzy blankets, pop the link into the chat window, and send him a quick message.

FlashPoint: *If you don't up your game, I'm going to tease you mercilessly for being the only SEAL alive who can't hit the broad side of an alien transpo with an assault rifle.*

That should shut him up for a while and give me time to think. Or avoid. Avoidance is easier. I head over to the Family and Relationships board. Fifteen new messages await—unsurprising, as families can be stressful under the best of circumstances. Add in PTSD, paralysis, amputation, and any of the other assorted injuries our members deal with, and you ratchet the stress level up to a thousand.

A new amputee, JT893, posts about his girlfriend walking out on him, and the other members pile on, offering the predictable-but-true "you can do better than her" platitudes. I agree. Amputees with proper care can do almost anything these days with the advances in prosthetics, and if this chick doesn't understand that, she doesn't deserve JT.

Over on the Rants and Vents board, a long thread catches my eye.

HuskyFan1998: *New here. I served for nine years and came back so FUBAR that I couldn't go back to my old job. Bummed around on my pension until my wife got pregnant, and then found this sweet job I loved. Great hours, enough money for us to get by, and paid vacation. And it all went to hell a month ago. The company started this big remodel and the noise... God, I thought I was back in Iraq. Jackhammers, nail guns, power sanders. I couldn't think straight. And then this customer starts yelling at me. Sounded just like my old CO. I lost it. Started to shake, barely stopped myself from pissing down my leg. I couldn't move. Couldn't think. When my boss came over, he jabbed me in the chest, and I swung at him. Missed, thank God. If I'd hit him, I'd probably be in jail.*

Getting fired sucks ass, and my wife's pregnant again. I can't support us on my army pension, and she's on bed rest. We're going to run out of savings soon. And then I come home today to find out that I can't borrow against my 401K because HR fucked up my paperwork. I needed that money to cover our health insurance until my new job's coverage kicks in at the end of the month. What the hell am I going to do? My boss just had to touch me. I should sue him for all he's worth. And the company too. They can't do this to me. My wife can barely stand to look at me, and my son keeps asking why Mommy cries all the time. I don't know what else to do.

HuskyFan1998 echoes the desperation a lot of us feel. Messed up after our tours, we try to put our lives back together, but some of us never do. I can't fix his problems, but sometimes we just need to know someone understands.

FlashPoint: *HuskyFan, I'm one of the moderators here. Just wanted to tell you that you're not alone. PTSD's no joke. Sounds like your boss is damn lucky he's never experienced it. I've got a list of lawyers in the greater Seattle area if that'd help. There might not be anything they can do—I know nothing about the law, really—but some of them take on pro bono work. At least they'd be able to tell you if there's anything they can do about your 401k.*

I wish I could offer more than sympathy. Stick around and get to know folks. Above all, what's posted here, stays here. Though we let anyone join, we take privacy very seriously. So vent all you want. I learned a long time ago that the worst thing you can do is keep your pain bottled up inside. Take care of yourself.

Oh, and go pick a fresh flower for your wife. Just one. You'd be surprised how much it helps both of you.

As I pile pizza on my plate, my right hand twinges with an electric pain—damn nerve damage stole the sensation in my last two fingers, and when I'm tired, spasms like this are common. I massage my forearm, willing the fire away, then turn on the Xbox.

"About time," West teases when I open the voice channel. "I'd started to worry you couldn't handle my superior battle skills."

I can't help snorting. "You mean your superior *dying* skills? Lock and load, frogman."

On screen, my heavily armored character hefts her gun. Smoke swirls around her as the music thuds an ominous beat. I flex my fingers on the controller, waiting for West to engage. His character joins mine, and before long, we're battling a horde of hostiles while we try to finish this quest.

"Take that, you piece of shit," West mutters an hour later as he takes out a sentry.

"Nice." I go after the next in the long line of foes. "You've been practicing. Cheating on me with another gamer? Or just lulling me into a false sense of security?"

He chuckles. "Never. You're the best partner I've ever had." On screen, he takes out a particularly nasty foe. "Booyah! Take that, you gorram scum."

Laughing, I launch an attack of my own. He's almost as geeky as I am, and we've had a couple long discussions about the eleventh Doctor Who's legacy and whether the final season of *Buffy* was awful or epic.

I shift in my chair, and my long-forgotten plate crashes to the floor, sending crumbs everywhere. I curse, forgetting to mute my headset.

"You okay?"

"Yeah," I answer through clenched teeth. "Need a minute." Hissing out a breath, I force my stiff muscles into action to clean up the mess. Exhaustion burns my eyes, and when I return to the game, I blink hard to focus. "I know it's early, but I haven't slept much lately. I'm going to call it a night."

"Wait." He pauses the game, and my screen dims. "Have coffee with me tomorrow."

My mouth suddenly feels like the Sahara, and I tug at the neck of my t-shirt. "Um, I'm not sure that's a good idea."

"Don't tell me you hate coffee. My heart couldn't take that." His slight hint of a drawl lends a gentleness to the words, and I wonder if he'd sound as sexy in person.

"I love coffee. My blood's caffeinated. But...we should stick to gaming. And VetNet. Keep things casual."

"Angel, we've been gaming together for weeks now. I think we've moved past casual."

There's no reason not to meet, other than that vague "this guy could be a serial killer" worry—and my irrational fear of having to be charming.

I don't do charming.

"Let me buy you a macchiato," he says. "Have you ever been to Broadcast Coffee?"

"Down on Pike?"

"Yep. Best coffee in Seattle. They roast their own beans and have this whole 'coffee tasting' experience. What do you usually drink?" The hope in his voice deepens his twang, making my insides melt just a little.

"I make an Americano every morning. Grocery store beans, though."

He coughs in disapproval. "Excuse me? I thought we were friends. Now you have to come. Just so you can taste what you're missing. Give me one cup of coffee to change your mind. If you don't have a good time, I'll never ask again."

Dammit. Coffee with a friend. That's not a date, right?

"I'll be there."

CAM

Caffeine-desperate patrons fill Broadcast Coffee. Conversations carry over the whir of the burr grinders, and the hiss of the steamer wands punctuate the grunge tunes on the speakers. I don't see an open table anywhere, and the idea of doing this "not-a-date" at the standing coffee bar has me glancing towards the exit. Then I notice a god in a blue t-shirt, and I try—unsuccessfully—to pick my chin up off the floor.

West holds up his hand, and the movement highlights the stars and stripes inked around his bicep. Praying I look more composed than I feel, I weave between the tables as he stands to greet me.

"Cam?" His lopsided grin almost puts me at ease. Except for the whole Adonis vibe he's got going on. Well over six feet tall, he's perfection in his Levi's and snug tee emphasizing his flat abs and broad chest. The kind of guy who can wink at a girl, and she'll melt at his feet.

His warm hand envelops mine, and dammit if I don't hold on a moment too long. He leans closer, as if he's going to kiss me, and I jerk back. But he's only reaching for my chair, and a blush heats my cheeks. "Thanks."

"No trouble finding the place?" Skimming a hand down my arm as he pulls away, he smiles again, and I try not to lose my words completely when he sits across from me.

"I only live a few blocks east. You come here often?"

"One of the guys from my dojo owns the place. He gave me shit for months when he saw a Siren to-go cup on my desk. Now I'm here every weekend." He runs a hand through his short-cropped hair, and I wonder if he's as nervous as I am.

"So...what's good? What should I order?"

"Do you trust me?" Azure eyes, a layer of stubble along an angular jaw, and a single scar that bisects his eyebrow are probably at the top of most women's fantasy scorecards. When my gaze lands on his lips, I force a deep breath. This man should be a model...and it's been a long time since I've been with anyone.

"Um...sure?" I dig a twenty out of my wallet, but he shakes his head.

"My treat."

Before I can protest, he ambles off, and I can't resist watching his ass and the way his back muscles shift under the t-shirt as he leans against the counter. Though my daily swims keep me reasonably fit, West is in another league. One that runs, lifts weights, and probably does CrossFit. On most days, I can't manage without my cane.

My right hand starts to tingle, and I curse. *Not now.* Stealing another glance at West, who's smiling and charming the barista, I squeeze my forearm. The thick scar from a white-hot piece of shrapnel has no sensation, but underneath, the muscle spasms painfully until I find the trigger point. Ink surrounds the worst of the troughs from the shrapnel, but no amount of flowers, stars, and doves can mask what happened.

By the time West returns, my hand's steady again, and as he deposits the tray between us, I gawk. "I love coffee, but two espressos and a latte? Each? Are you trying to keep me up all night?"

He winks, and my stomach does a little somersault. "Maybe."

When will I learn to think before I open my mouth? Then again, it's not like I've had a lot of practice flirting lately. "So… uh…what is all this?"

"Two different espressos—one from Guatemala and one from Indonesia. That's the coffee tasting."

"And the latte?" I quirk an eyebrow.

"That's not a latte."

"Then what is it?" I eye the "latte," suddenly unsure I have any right to call myself a coffee addict. A dark brown heart drawn in the foam slowly spreads as the tiny bubbles burst.

"Delicious." He nudges a glass of water towards me. "There's a whole ritual around the tasting. Adam, the guy who owns the place, walked me through it my first time. Before we start, cleanse your palate with the sparkling water."

"Okay." I lift the glass to my lips, and he mirrors my movement. The bubbles burst over my tongue, and I can't look away from his intense gaze. Squirming in my seat, I wonder what he'd taste like—or look like without that t-shirt. *Stop it, Delgado. This isn't a date.*

Even I don't believe my own bullshit anymore.

"The best flavors are at the bottom of the cup." He picks up a spoon the size of his pinky and gives the first shot of espresso a little stir.

Desperate for any distraction, I try to follow along, but maneuvering this tiny utensil in a cup the size of a golf ball proves a devilish task, and as I slosh espresso over the rim, my embarrassment rises, threatening to bubble over. How the hell is he so graceful?

"Now slurp the espresso." My face must show my disbelief because he chuckles. "You said you trusted me, remember?"

I did.

When West lifts his espresso cup, I do the same, and I'm surprised at the strong chocolaty scent that wafts from the dark brew. Though I feel ridiculous slurping coffee like a two-year-old, the taste shocks me. Far from just coffee, I pick out several distinct flavors.

"This is really good."

His lips twitch into a half-smile, and his shoulders relax. "What did you taste?"

"Orange, chocolate, and...butterscotch."

He nods. "Try the other cup?"

I have a harder time with this one, only able to give him a vague "candy" description when I'm done, and as he reads off the flavor notes he got from the barista, I'm drawn to his lips, how they move, wondering how that stubble would rasp against my skin.

He finishes his second espresso and leans back in his chair. "How long have you lived in Seattle?"

"Eight years. I moved up here after I got out of rehab down in Los Angeles. I couldn't stand the idea of going back to Modesto—and my family—but that's a long story."

He cocks his head, and the movement highlights his broad shoulders. "I've got time."

No one needs to hear about my foolish teenage years or the shit that went down right before I joined the army. Especially not on a first...whatever the hell this is. I shake my head. "I'd need alcohol. A lot of alcohol."

"Does that mean you'll have dinner with me soon?"

If my mouth is full of coffee, I won't have to answer, right? I down the rest of the espresso like a shot of vodka, but he's leaning forward now, waiting for my reply.

Distraction. I need a distraction, right now. "So, uh...you own your dojo, right? How many classes a week do you teach?"

Tiny lines tighten around his lips for a second before he clears his throat. "Not so many these days. I spend most of my time on paperwork and advertising."

"Do you miss it—the teaching?"

"Every damn day." Longing deepens his twang, and he rubs the back of his neck. I've touched a nerve, and I don't know how to soothe the raw spot.

"West—"

He shifts his gaze to the "not-a-latte" in front of me. "Broadcast is famous for their macchiatos. Try it."

"I don't like sweet drinks." He frowns, and I try to stifle my cringe. Sometimes, I don't even realize what's coming out of my mouth until the words emerge and I've offended someone. This probably-a-date may prove to be disastrous at the rate I'm going.

"This isn't sweet." His tone carries an edge. "It's a shot of espresso and just enough steamed milk to mellow the bitterness."

The mug rests heavy in my hand. Before I can take a sip, a guy a few tables away knocks over his chair, and the loud *crack* makes me jump. My fingers spasm and the cup crashes to the floor, sending pieces of ceramic skittering across the hardwood. Hot coffee splatters my shirt, my jeans, and my right shoe. "Dammit!" I lean down to try to pick up the broken cup handle, but off balance and flustered, I slip off the chair and onto my ass.

"Fuck, Cam." West leaps out of his own chair, then slides his hands under my arms, which only serves to deepen my embarrassment, and when he lifts me, I try to twist away. "Relax, angel. I've got you." He helps me back into my chair. "Are you okay?"

The pity swirling in his eyes raises my defenses. "Fine."

West pauses for a beat before he mutters something about napkins and rushes off to the counter.

"Dammit." Coffee squishes as I wiggle my toes, and as I glance down, the brown stain just below my breast makes me want to take a backhoe to the now-stained floor and dig a hole big enough to crawl into.

The barista rushes over, and she and West clean up the mess. I wrestle my phone out of my bag and then fiddle with the screen, engaging my backup plan—a work emergency.

West wipes his hands on his jeans and then stands. "I'll get you another macchiato."

"I have to go. Work...needs me." Offering what I hope is an apologetic smile, I slide my cane off the back of the chair. "Thank you for the coffee, but—"

West reaches for my hand. "Stay. Please. At least for another cup of coffee."

"I can't, West. I'm sorry. I'm a mess—literally."

"You're beau—"

"Some people are just better online. We should stick with fighting aliens and binge watching *Doctor Who*." In the tight space, I brush the table with my hip as I stand, the empty espresso cups rattling in their saucers, West's untouched macchiato sloshing over the ceramic rim, leaving a milky stain on the dark wood. He steadies me, his hands on my hips. His uncertain expression tempts me to stay, to wipe the slate clean and start over.

But if I do, I'll spend every minute self-conscious, tugging at my stained shirt, and he'll ogle—what man wouldn't?—until I can't face him ever again. I won't be able to salvage the friendship we've formed, and while I can tell he wants more, I can't even get through coffee; there's no way I could make it through an actual date.

"I'm sorry." Slipping out of his grasp, I weave my way around the tables, and when I pause steps from the exit, I can feel his stare. I can't look back. I won't. And yet, as the heavy glass door closes between us, I relent and meet his gaze.

The confusion etched on his face almost sends me back inside, but I made my choice. I shake my head as a final apology and then head for home.

WEST

The barista meets my gaze across the crowded shop and mouths "I'm sorry." Yeah, darlin'. So am I. Replaying the date in my head, I try to figure out where I went wrong. Pushing for dinner? Cam's an army explosives specialist—or was. A dinner invite shouldn't have sent her scurrying. We've spent almost every damn night talking, gaming, and flirting since I discovered VetNet six weeks ago.

A splash of coffee mars the table next to my macchiato. The broken mug? She wouldn't look me in the eyes after that.

"Do what I do. Hold tight and pretend it's a plan." One of her favorite *Doctor Who* quotes. Well, I had a plan. Get her to agree to dinner. For weeks now, she's driven me half-crazy with her irreverent mouth and her uncanny ability to predict right when we're going to be ambushed by a horde of aliens.

The week we binge-watched *Firefly* together while conquering Mass Effect did me in. I had to meet her. Had to know if I'd feel a spark. Now, I'm on fire, and she's gone. Despite her insistence that we stick to gaming, I can't walk away, so I pull out my phone.

Cam, whatever I did, I'm sorry. Please call me.

My macchiato's lukewarm now, so I carry the tray to the counter and then unload it with a little more force than strictly necessary. A few hours on the heavy bag will erase the memory of the morning, right? And put out these flames? Yeah, even I don't believe that.

"HOLY SHIT."

The man leaning against the corner of Lakeview Krav Maga wears an expression somewhere between boredom and irritation, but at my curse, he breaks into a wide smile.

"About fucking time, Sampson. You've heard of this thing called 'work'?" He pushes off the wall, then claps me on the back hard enough to make me cough. "Your website said you were teaching the morning advanced session. I've been out here for two hours."

"Yeah, well the Saturday morning sessions are on hold indefinitely. What the hell are you doing here, Ry?" I'm wound tight enough to snap without warning, and given the look in Ryker's grey eyes, this isn't a social call.

"There somewhere private we can talk?"

Ryker McCabe, the only man to bust out of Hell Mountain—the system of caves east of Fallujah where the most valuable POWs were hidden and tortured—has more in common with a piece of granite than a man, but he saved my life twice in a matter of hours, so I overlook the fact that the last time we saw each other, I told him to fuck off. Jerking my thumb towards the dojo door, I mutter, "My office."

He's too big to comfortably settle into the guest chair—six-foot-eight, at least two-fifty, and solid muscle under his scars. Insurgents tortured him within an inch of his life for two years, and there's not a patch of skin unmarked except the left side of his face. Fuckers wanted him to remember he'd been a good looking guy once. He leans against my closed door, and I slide a hip onto my desk. "You'd better not be here on a recruiting mission."

"West, you're the best damn infiltration specialist I've ever seen. Coop's got great reflexes, but he doesn't have your instincts, and Inara's too valuable as a sharpshooter. That leaves me." He gestures towards the scarred side of his face. "My undercover days ended in Hell."

"What about Landow?"

"Dead." Ryker stares down at his polished Doc Martins. "Goddamn fucking drunk driver cut him down outside of HQ three days before we were supposed to head to the Sudan. We need you."

"There are dozens of former SEALs, Rangers—"

"None of them have your skills. Two missions a month—tops. Base rate is five large, just for getting on the plane. Hazard pay for anything in a war zone." Ryker rubs his meaty palm over his bald head. His right eye droops—nerve damage—and the mangled lid makes him look perpetually sad. "At least come meet the team."

"No." The word catches in my throat. Five thousand dollars for a couple days' work is hard to turn down, and as I look away from

Ryker's hard stare, I catch sight of the loan paperwork sitting on the corner of my desk. I left that life eight years ago, and I still wake in a cold sweat more nights than not, the scent of blood in my nose, my team's screams in my ears, and the image of the broken body of an innocent Afghan grandmother burned into the inside of my eyelids.

"West?" Ryker's voice drops. "You'd be saving innocent lives."

Shaking my head to banish the memories, I clear my throat. "I'll make some calls. I've got a couple of buddies who'd be good at K&R."

Ryker grunts what might be another curse, then yanks my door open. As he crosses the threshold, he pauses but doesn't turn around. "You change your mind, you know where to find me."

3

CAM

*a*lone in the office, I turn up the music. P!nk never fails to raise my spirits, but today, Pandora favors love songs.

"Get over it," I mutter as I load up one of Oversight's modules. "You don't have time for this sappy bullshit. You don't even like him in that way." Jabbing my phone screen—and completely ignoring the text message waiting there—I switch the music to an instrumental dance station. Pandora should really have a "bad date" setting.

"Come on, baby," I whisper to my code. "Let's see if you can cheer me up."

Two hours later, my mood hasn't improved. I made the mistake of looking at the schematics for the camera wiring LaCosta's head of security sent over—and to my shock, discovered Royce had picked up a copy last week. Their old system ran on Wi-Fi. Ours is hard-wired. We'll have to run all new cable. They've got a relay switch that'll mess with our electrical plans, and some of the conduits are too damn small. With the accelerated schedule, installing two hundred and fifteen state-of-the-art hookups with battery backups is going to run us well over deadline. Once I send an emergency text to Royce, I head for the conference room.

On the white board, I start to sketch out a revised schedule. Every date I ink on the wall ratchets my stress level more. Royce is going to have to do something. Oversight's my baby, but he's the one who took this commission—and then stuck me in LaCosta's office alone knowing we needed to cable the whole damn hotel.

He lumbers in as I cap the dry erase marker and survey my work. "This couldn't wait until Monday?"

If I beat him with my cane, I'll be out of a job. Still, I find myself tightening my grip on the handle, relying on the familiar curves and grooves to settle my nerves. When I force my gaze up, Royce's exhaustion shocks me. "You okay, Rolls?"

"We agreed you wouldn't call me that anymore."

"We also agreed you'd show up to the meeting yesterday. Instead, you leave me alone to deal with the change in schedule and don't return my calls. I picked up a copy of the schematics this morning—and then found out you've had them for a week and didn't say anything. You backed me—and this whole company— against a wall. Had I known the parking garage was six levels with no CAT-5, I never would have agreed to the accelerated date. There's no way we can get the work done before Labor Day. We've got two people to cable twenty floors, the parking garage, and the rooftop deck."

Royce runs a hand through his messy brown hair. "How many people do you need?"

I shrug. "This job is at least twice the size of anything we've done before. My best guess? Six. Ask the installer you hired. What's his name?"

"Al. I'll call him. Pretty sure he was finishing up one of the residential jobs today."

I follow Royce into his office. Coffee cups litter his desk, and the scent of stale take-out lingers. A stack of files next to his computer leans precariously, so unlike the organized lieutenant I served with.

Royce leaves a message for Al, then he sinks back in his chair. "Lucas can help with cabling. I'll find a way to pull in a few more guys. Al might know of some, and if not, I'll bring in some temps first thing Monday morning."

I turn to go, but Royce calls after me. "We can't mess this one up, Cam."

No shit. "We won't. But you've got to keep me in the loop." My voice cracks, and I clear my throat. Not today. I can't go there today. "I'm headed home. I'll check with Lucas tomorrow. Maybe he can get started after brunch."

"They'll be a couple of comp days in it for both of you." Royce's shoulders hunch as he reaches for his keyboard.

He looked better crawling through the Afghan desert at three in the morning than he does right now. I swallow around the lump in my throat. "You okay?"

Royce opens his mouth, then seems to think better of his words and nods his head before returning his focus to his computer. Whatever moment we'd been about to share slips through my grasp, like so many others since that hot day in April ten years ago.

HuskyFan1988: *How did you know about the flower?*

HuskyFan's message brings a smile after this trying day. Two texts from West headline my inbox, but I ignore them and reply to HuskyFan instead. At least this I can't screw up.

FlashPoint: *Most women don't want to be given the world. They want to know that their partners think about them during the day. That no matter what else is going on, they matter. When you pick her a flower, you're giving her a piece of your heart. Not your paycheck, your health insurance, or even your ability to lift heavy objects. Surprise her with a flower or a little Post-It note or even just a kiss whenever she's down. I hope things turn around for you soon, buddy.*

Seconds later, a new message waits for me.

HuskyFan1988: *Sounds like you've been on the receiving end of more than one flower.*

If only...

FlashPoint: *My father used to pick daisies for my mother. Probably still does. I didn't inherit his romantic instincts. Couldn't even manage a first date this morning without screwing things up.*

I don't know why I shared that failure with someone I don't even know, but a small wisp of the black cloud over my head fades a little with the admission.

HuskyFan1988: *You probably didn't screw up as badly as you think. What happened?*

FlashPoint: *I dumped coffee down my shirt and then landed on my ass trying to pick up the shattered pieces of the mug off the floor.*

HuskyFan1988: *So?*

FlashPoint: *He...*

I stare at the blinking cursor. What the hell can I say? He tried to help me up? I can't look him in the eyes because I'm scared he only sees the broken parts of me? West didn't *do* anything wrong. I did.

HuskyFan1988: *You helped me, so let me give you some advice. Us guys spend most of our lives convinced women are goddesses and we're not worthy. A woman who swears, breaks coffee mugs, and can laugh off an embarrassing stain? You can probably do no wrong in his book. Be honest. Tell him you screwed up and give him another chance.*

Score two for me. Unfortunately, I failed at the honesty part. Miserably.

Without the promise of West as my companion in the alien-laden game land, the evening drags on. This morning's cowardice leaves a bad taste in my mouth—or perhaps that's the rubbery noodles and pasty cheese from my over-nuked lasagna. My eyes burn the longer I work, and a little after ten, I yield to the growing heaviness of my lids and trudge to the bedroom.

After some yoga stretching to alleviate the tightness in my hip, I curl under the blankets with a book—an old science fiction paper-back with weathered pages and a cracked spine that's seen better days. Two chapters in, my buzzing phone pulls me from the vortex of deep space.

West: *You weren't online tonight. Talk to me, Cam. It was just coffee. Not a marriage proposal.*

I can't. Not now. Not when the memory of his hands on me is still so vivid. My attempts to return to my book fail miserably as his words echo. *"Fuck, Cam. I've got you."*

No one "gets me." I can "get myself," thank you very much.

4

CAM

*S*unday morning dawns clear and warm, and the outdoor deck at Ray's buzzes with conversation. I drop into a chair across from Lucas. We have a standing brunch date once a month—open to the whole company, though Lucas and I are the only constants.

The clatter of silverware overshadows the conversations around us as it seems half of Seattle decided to dine outside this morning. Lucas slumps in his seat. "I ordered you the usual."

Maybe a bloody mary will smooth away the regrets that haunted me all night. Otherwise, this is going to be a long brunch. "Luc, I've got a…" My jaw drops. "Holy shit."

Royce weaves between the tables, a dour expression etched on his face.

"Haven't seen you at one of these in a while, Rol—Royce."

"I'm tired of the two of you riding my ass on Monday mornings. This should earn me at least a year's peace." Royce opens his menu with a snap. "You give me shit, and I'm out of here."

Lucas and I exchange glances, and I shrug. For two weeks, I've waited for Royce to get over his latest dark mood, but Mr. Prickly appears to be here to stay. "Fair enough."

Royce doesn't look up from his menu, and the thick paper crumples in his grip as the server arrives to take his order.

Well, this is awkward. Lucas and I stare at one another, and we both shrug at the same time.

Royce doesn't seem to notice the tension as he pulls out his phone. Whatever's on the screen is a hell of a lot more interesting than anything at the table, and I clench my jaw so hard my teeth hurt. Only the drink delivery saves me from cracking a molar.

"Hooah." We toast, and I almost choke from the spice. "All right. Hand over my 'no heat' mary, Luc."

Lucas shudders and passes me his glass. "How do you drink them like this? That's straight tomato juice."

"Wimp, remember?" I point to myself and smile, then glance at Royce. He's staring out over the glittering waters of Elliot Bay, his phone still in his hand, oblivious to our exchange. "Earth to Royce. Come in, Lieutenant." He barely acknowledges me, and I snap. "Dammit, Royce. What the hell is up with you?" A little old lady with snow-white hair shushes me from the next table, and I lower my voice. "Everyone in the office has noticed. You're coming in late, leaving early, and you never say more than two or three words to anyone unless you're riding their asses for something. Take that stick out of your ass and talk to me."

Lucas sucks down his bloody mary and motions for another. I'm tempted to do the same, but I'm worried. Despite Royce's determination to keep me at arm's length since I got blown up, serving together forged a bond that can't be broken. I've let him push me away for too long, and every time, he tears another chunk from my armor. No more.

"You're on thin ice, Cam." Royce twists his napkin, and the edge to his voice should warn me away, but after my awful weekend, I'm in the mood for a fight.

"You built a damn fine company. One we're all proud to be a part of. But if you're not careful, you're going to lose everything.

Orion said you laid into him on Tuesday because he didn't refill the coffee pot. And Abbie caught you kicking the vending machine. You know that shit triggers her. I love you, Royce. But you've been an asshole for two weeks."

Royce stares down at his hands, the napkin shredded on the table in front of him. For a moment, I think I see his fingers tremble. "I know."

"Are you going to talk to me?" I lean closer, reaching for his hand.

He yanks his arm away. Digging in his pocket, he pulls out his wallet. The twenty floats onto the table as he stands and glowers down at me.

"I got us a contract with ZoomWare." As I gasp, he gives me a curt nod. "Exactly. I'm making you lead. But they won't sign until the Coana job's done and Phillip LaCosta is happy. You want to know why I'm pissed off? Stressed out all the time? Because if we fuck up Coana, this company's through. You have no idea how hard it is to have everyone's future in my hands. I don't come to these meetups because I spend all my time trying to keep the firm afloat. Give me a break and do your damn job." And with that, he turns on his heel and strides away, nearly bowling over the server with our food.

Lucas takes a long pull on his second drink, and I join him. "I knew he had a client meeting on Thursday, but ZoomWare?"

"Doesn't explain the past two weeks. Dude needs medication. Or something. I know you love the guy, Cam, but he's going to implode soon, and I worry we're all going to be sucked down with him."

Lucas isn't wrong. I run a hand through my dark locks, trying to come up with a response that doesn't sound like an excuse. "He's hurting. I don't know why, or what triggered it, but he's dealing with something heavy."

"You served with him. What's his deal?"

"Hell if I know. Once I got hurt, Royce joined a new squad. He's never talked about what happened on his last tour. Never talked about anything after that, really. This isn't the Royce I knew."

I dig into my stack of pancakes, and Lucas reaches for Royce's untouched plate of bacon to add to his already impressive omelet. As he shakes hot sauce onto his eggs, he glances over at me. "I could say the same about you."

"What?" I pause with a forkful of pancakes dripping syrup onto my plate.

"Something about you feels off. And don't tell me you slept like shit. I can see that. You need some heavy-duty concealer to cover up those suitcases under your eyes. What's wrong?"

The problem with knowing someone for six years? Working with them every day? It's almost impossible to bullshit them. "Bad date yesterday."

"Camilla Maria Delgado, why didn't you tell me?" He nudges my shoulder before he returns to his massive plate of food.

"Because of this reaction. We had coffee. Hell, it was barely a date. And given how it ended, there won't be a repeat performance." I dredge a forkful of pancake through a lake of maple syrup, wishing I hadn't dropped that mug, hadn't run out on West without any explanation. "Leave it alone. I'm moving on."

"Nope. You've got that 'I fucked up' look, and I want to know why." He rests his elbows on the table, folds his hands, and cradles his chin. "Talk."

I can't resist Lucas when he's in therapist mode. And deep down, I need to tell someone. When I finish recounting the whole morning—and the emails and text messages West sent me afterwards, all of them as yet unanswered—Lucas clucks his tongue.

"Honey, you fucked up big time. The poor man mopped up a macchiato, offered to buy you another, and you think he doesn't like you because you made a mess?"

"Well, when you put it that way…" I shove the half-full plate of pancakes away. "We've known each other almost two months, game together most nights. But five minutes sitting across a table from him, and I felt like I was back in high school, going to

Denny's on a first date, all nervous optimism and anticipation. He's hot. Did I mention that? And he can quote *Firefly*. And *Doctor Who*."

I drop my gaze to my lap when I realize I'm gushing, which only makes Lucas chuckle.

"You need to call that man back ASAP." He rests a hand on his hip and arches a brow. "Don't make me steal your phone and text him myself."

I shake my head. "Dating a man who looks like he belongs on the cover of *Men's Health* isn't my speed. The last three guys I dated were vets with serious injuries: a prosthetic arm, a missing leg, and, hell, Efron got burned in a Humvee crash. We matched, you know?"

Lucas nods, then sighs—a mother hen disappointed in his chick. "Honey, I've seen you do things with code that shouldn't be possible. For all your loner bravado, you'll do anything for the people you're close to. And you're gorgeous." He waves his hand at me. "All that hair, your perfect skin, those tats... You're a catch for any man. If I didn't bat for the other team, I'd be all over you."

I can't help laughing, and I feel lighter than I have since I ruined the "of-course-it-was-a-date" yesterday morning. "I love you too, Lucas. Sometimes, I think you're the only one who gets me."

"I've got your back." He jabs my arm. "Even when you're being an idiot. Lighten up on yourself, Cam. Have some fun. I doubt your hot SEAL wanted to propose marriage. Call him back. Apologize."

Lucas is right. He's always right—at least where other people's relationships are concerned. As I sip the last of my bloody mary—sans Tabasco—I stare out over the water. I missed chatting with West last night. And I have only myself to blame.

UNLIKE YESTERDAY, Broadcast's lonely tables beg for patrons this afternoon. A single barista leans against the counter, a book in her hand.

"*A Midsummer Night's Dream*? One of my favorites." I smile, then glance up at the board listing the various coffee offerings. Espressos, lattes, the illustrious macchiato, and the coffee tasting "experience." I'm used to Siren Coffee's menu, full of overly sweet drinks: pumpkin pie lattes, s'mores mochas and the like. This place might just grow on me. Assuming I fix things with West.

Barista girl stows the book in her apron, smiling. "What'll you have?"

"One macchiato to go, please. Almond milk."

She turns to the grinder, pulls a handle four times, and sets the espresso shot to brew. "Good choice. We make the best in town."

As the espresso brews, I stare at the table we shared and remember the feel of his fingers on mine, the heat of his skin as he steadied me when I tried to run, and the disappointment on his face as I walked out the door.

Her foot taps to the beat of the reggae blasting through the speakers, and as Third World belts out the lyrics to "Now That We Found Love," I pull out my phone to read West's messages again.

Why didn't we stick to our online flirting? Something shifted between us when we met, and I don't know if we can go back to what we were—to the friendship we'd formed over geeky television shows and gaming. My stomach flips when I realize I don't want to. Sitting across from him, seeing the possibility for something more…something real…

A dull ache settles in my thigh. Brunch and three errands in one day? Not smart. Though I can't wait to go home and lie down with my leg up, I have one thing to do first. I snap a photo of the macchiato and spend a full five minutes trying to come up with an eloquent apology. After a lot of backspacing, I go for short and simple.

I screwed up. I'm sorry.

West didn't lie: the macchiato isn't sweet. The milk lends a gentleness, a comforting depth to the espresso that I didn't expect, and though I'm strangling my phone, hoping he'll reply, I smile.

But the phone mocks me with silence the whole way home. Not until I settle in my recliner with a pain pill dulling the edges of the world does the phone start to vibrate off the table.

"I'm an idiot," I say as I settle back against the cushions with a wince. "I panicked."

"No shit. I didn't think you were the type."

Right to the point. I can't say I blame him. Closing my eyes, I search for my next words. I've had this conversation in my head a dozen times in the past hour, but every time, it ends with us never speaking to one another again.

Give me an IED or a land mine, and I do fine. But put me in front of a man I like, and I turn into an insecure mess. "I'm not. But I saw how you looked at me when I dropped the macchiato. I don't want your pity, West."

His frustration carries over the line. "Pity? You were in pain. On the floor. Was I supposed to just leave you there?"

I don't have a smart reply. Or any reply.

"You don't know me well enough yet to judge whether I'm pitying you or was simply worried that you landed on your ass when I know you have a bad hip. I didn't give a shit about the macchiato. Life is full of broken mugs.

"You bolted after fifteen minutes. And then you ignored my messages, didn't log on to play *Halo* last night. Avoidance isn't your style. At least not the Cam I've gotten to know the past few weeks."

Score another point for West. If I don't level up in my apology skill, this conversation is over. "I'm sorry, okay? Can we go back to being friends? Playing Xbox in the evenings and complaining about the wait for the next gen console?"

"I want more."

My breath catches in my throat, and I stammer, "M-more?"

"I like you, Cam. And yesterday, right before it all went to hell,

I met someone I want to know better. Someone I want to date. And I think you felt the same. Am I wrong?"

I want to answer him. But my cowardice gets in the way, and he loses patience.

"I won't chase you, angel. I'm not that kind of guy. If you want to run away, that's your choice. I'm glad you finally got to have a macchiato. I hope it didn't disappoint you like I did."

As the line falls silent, I tally up the score. And the big, fat goose egg in my column doesn't surprise me. I don't do charming. Obviously, I don't do apologies very well either.

5

WEST

I need to hit something. Stripping out of my t-shirt, I eye the heavy bags. Eight of them line the far wall of the studio. Once upon a time, I had students in here twelve hours a day, training, working out, laughing and sparring with one another. These days, we might as well be closed on Sundays. And Saturdays. And some Thursdays.

A heavy bass beat thunders from the CrossFit studio across the street. I recognize some of the cars in their lot. Former students of mine. Using my teeth to tighten the velcro strap on my second glove, I glare at their sign. *Cross Your Fit* blazes in red letters with silhouettes of two of the fittest people on the planet behind the words.

Thwack. The first hit sends the bag swinging, and I wait for its arc to stabilize before I go back in for a combo. "Fucking spin classes." CYF's latest offering tempted another four of my regulars to jump ship. Sure, they still pay for the occasional one-off class here and there, but those sweet membership fees are long gone. Frustration spurs me to punch harder, faster, and soon, I'm in the zone.

"Hi, boss," Vasquez calls as he bounds through the front door. "Dead again?"

I turn and arch a brow. "Hey, Captain Obvious. Make yourself useful." Another hard set of combos send vibrations up my arms, and sweat beads down the center of my back as Vasquez takes his spot behind the bag, providing me some much needed stability so I can push myself harder. "Don't know…if you'll have…a full class."

I've slacked on my bag skills lately. Too much paperwork. My biceps start to burn, my thighs tremble as I reach the half-hour mark, and my abs shake from the exertion. When Vasquez pops his head to the side and then nods towards the clock on the wall, I drop my hands.

"You all right, boss?" He picks up a spray bottle and towel and then starts to wipe down the bag as I pull off my gloves.

"Never better." The lie slips out easily, though I doubt I'm convincing. The dojo's in trouble, I can't keep up with the bills, and the most interesting woman I've met in years doesn't know how to talk to me. "I'm headed home for the day. Have a good class."

"Get some rest, boss. You look like shit."

———

BEER AND SHUTOUT baseball should distract me, but in the silent spaces between pitches, there's only Cam—or a sharp, witty, and gorgeous Cam-shaped hole. We should be chatting on VetNet or blasting hostiles online while the game plays on the radio. I didn't realize how much she'd come to mean to me in six short weeks, or how often we'd text one another for no reason at all, then end up chatting for hours. I close my eyes, letting the droning of the announcers lull me into the space between asleep and awake.

Blood. The scent fills my nose, so thick and cloying I can't breathe. My shoulder's on fire, and try as I might, I can't move my arm. Smitty stares from a few feet away, his skull dented, his eyes dilated in the shock of sudden death. Screams bounce off the clay and stone walls until I can't think, can't do anything but pray someone will get us out before the next missile hits.

My throat burns when I jerk awake, the screams in my nightmare echoing in the here and now. Sweat plasters my t-shirt to my chest, and my eyes feel hollow, my cheeks wet and clammy.

"Fuck." Every time I think I've beaten the nightmares, they shock me into humility. Losing most of my team, the grandmother and infant girl who perished alongside us, and my own weakness haunt me, and though my therapist tells me I'm doing fine, there are days I think he's full of shit.

My phone's in my hand before I even realize what I'm doing, and I have a message from Cam starting back at me—along with her address.

You didn't disappoint me—I disappointed myself. I'd like to apologize in person. Maybe then I won't screw it up.

CAM

By 5 p.m., I still haven't heard from him, and I'm contemplating dinner options and an early bedtime. At least asleep I won't have to keep staring at my silent phone. But the doorbell rings as I'm thumbing through takeout menus. "Hang on!"

My hunger—at least for food—takes a back seat when I open the door. West's t-shirt—green this time—turns his eyes a brilliant aquamarine, and a hint of aftershave reminds me of hiking through the Sierra Nevada foothills after a rainstorm—back before the bombs when I was free and whole. He holds up a bag from my favorite Thai restaurant, and in his other hand, he's got a six-pack of beer.

Nervousness settles in my belly. He's here, with food. But the serious expression etched on his face doesn't say "you're forgiven." I try for a smile. "How'd you know about Thai Ocean?"

He looks baffled. "I pay attention. You talked about this place last week. Can I come in?"

I nod, unable to come up with anything eloquent to say, and step aside.

He heads for my kitchen. While he arranges the takeout containers, I slide past him, intending to retrieve plates and glasses. But the narrow galley leaves little room, and he turns to face me, the heat in his gaze rooting me to the spot.

"I'm sorry," I whisper and lift a tentative hand to cup the back of his neck. I might not get another chance for this, and I have to know. Pulling him closer, I kiss him, and he wraps his arms around my waist. His tongue teases against the seam of my lips, and I open for him, heat flooding my core. As his hands roam upwards, his fingers tangling in my hair, I let him take, and I surrender to arousal so strong, I'd rip his clothes off if I thought he'd let me.

When he pulls away, his voice is strained. "Sit down. I'll get this."

If he's trying to punish me, he's doing a damn good job. I grab a beer to stop from licking my lips, to taste him lingering there because I'll only want more. The microbrew washes down my longing, and I stare out the window, the glittering diamonds of Puget Sound duller now that we're at odds. I can't help watching him as he sets the plates down and makes a production of separating his chopsticks.

"All right. I'm here. Talk." He examines a fresh roll as I push the pad thai around on my plate.

The warm breeze from my open patio door tickles my cheek, and I drag my fork through crumbled peanuts, searching for the right words.

Frantic to fill the silence, I blurt out the first thing that comes to mind. "We've spent almost every night together since we met—virtually. And every day, I'm glued to the clock, anticipating our next gaming session, but while Halo's a blast, *you're* the real reason I log on. To talk to someone who understands me, who laughs at my stupid jokes, and who brings over takeout and beer because he 'pays attention.'"

"So why can't we see where this goes? What about me is so scary you won't even consider it?"

Desperate for a minute to think, to come up with something worthy of this man in front of me, I shove a large bite of noodles into my mouth. And with it, a pepper. As the spice hits the back of my throat, I start to gag, and the battle to swallow brings tears to my eyes.

"Breathe, angel." West springs from his chair and slides his arm around me, his palm resting flat against my stomach. "Can you answer me?"

My nose is running now, and I can only manage short noisy breaths. But I nod, swallow after another exhale, and reach for my beer. He's still so close, his heat branding my back, and as he releases me, the absence of his touch leaves me with a shudder. "Sorry." The word rasps over my raw throat, and my cheeks catch fire as I push the plate away. "Give me a minute."

I lurch to my feet, and after a few awkward steps, I lean against the kitchen counter and try to compose myself. Will we ever have an easy conversation? Once I've stopped sniffling, I take a moment to study him from the door jamb. He's tense, his hands balled into fists at his sides. I rejoin him at the table. "I'm probably the only Mexican you'll ever meet who hates spicy food."

His eyes widen, and he slaps his hand over his heart. "Way to wound a guy, Cam. Now you'll never go to Szechuan Noodle House with me."

The promise of another date coaxes a smile as I shake my head. "Never. Lucas took me there for my birthday two years ago. I spent the whole meal crying into my ma po tofu. Even their one-star spice is too much for me. I haven't let him pick a restaurant since."

West chuckles. Despite my reservations about starting something, the fact that we can share a light moment despite recent disasters says a lot about his personality. Something's shifted between us, and my next words are easier, lighter.

"I didn't know how to explain." I turn my right hand palm up on the table. The deep, jagged scar that runs up my wrist doesn't hurt, but I feel the repercussions every day. "I don't have any sensation in my last two fingers. Sometimes, they have a mind of their own. Then when I couldn't even keep my ass in the chair…"

West takes my hand and squeezes. "That's all you had to say. Or hell, accidents happen. You didn't have to explain at all. But you still haven't answered my question. Why did you run away?"

"I don't know." He frowns, and I rush to fix yet another foible. "Maybe because it was easier to run away than have to watch another guy decide I'm too much trouble—too broken or too slow or too…me. I didn't understand that we couldn't go back to being just friends. Or that…I didn't want to."

West rises and moves to stare out the patio doors. His shoulders hike up around his ears, and he shoves his hands into his pockets. "I overreacted on the phone today."

"Maybe we both did."

With a sigh, he turns back to me. Small lines of strain bracket his lips, and his eyes darken. "My last girlfriend broke up with me after two years together. She said I'd disappointed her one too many times. But…I didn't understand what I'd done—or hadn't done. I'm a guy. We fuck up. Something on the Y-chromosome makes us oblivious to what's right in front of us. So when I heard that same tone in your voice, I got defensive."

I hold out my hand, and West links his fingers with mine. "Why don't we start over? You wanted to have dinner. We're having dinner. The rest…let's just see where things go."

"I'd like that." He tugs me against him, and for several seconds, I'm not the broken girl, the awkward girl, I'm the girl I used to be.

Before long, we're joking our way through our mango sticky

rice. He tells me about his older brother, Clay, and the teasing Clay suffered at the hands of the other kids.

"Our parents wanted us to be 'distinguished.' So his full name is Barclay Ulysses Sampson. Try surviving fifth grade as 'Barclay.' After the third bloody nose—on the other kid, not Clay—Mom and Dad sent us to another school where he got to be Clay, and I went by West."

"Wait. What's your real name, then?" I polish off my beer, and he pops the top on another, but doesn't hand the bottle over.

"If you laugh, I'm keeping this beer." Once I promise I won't, he pins me with a hard stare. "Westley Filbert Sampson."

My chuckle escapes before I can clap my hand over my mouth, and he takes a swig of the beer—my beer—as I fight for control.

"Filbert?" I snort. "Your parents must have hated you."

"That's Clay's theory. I'm pretty sure they were just rebelling against their own parents. At least my mom's. My grandmother named her Radiance Pearl. She legally changed her name to Rachel after college."

"If it makes you feel any better," I say, "the Princess Bride was one of my favorite movies growing up." I wiggle my fingers, demanding my beer, and he makes a show over debating whether or not I deserve the bottle.

"As you wish," he says as he presses the beer into my palm, then rises and picks up our plates. "Your turn. What embarrassing stories do you have from your childhood?"

"When I was eight, my best friend and I discovered Wonder Woman. We used to 'fly' around the neighborhood in our invisible jet with our magic bracelets made out of cardboard. I think we 'saved' all the boys at least once before they got tired of us and started running in the other direction. My parents grounded the invisible jet after we yelled at Mrs. Henderson for not seeing the plane and crushing it with her car."

With a fresh beer in his hand, West leans against the door jamb. "Are you close? To your parents?"

I press my lips together, then sigh. "No. Not anymore." He

waits for me to explain, and I scramble to shut his questions down. "Things got...complicated around the time I joined the army. Still are. Not something I like to talk about."

For a few seconds, only the traffic noises filtering up from the street break the silence. Then West clears his throat. "We made it through dinner. What's next?"

Thankful for the reprieve, I gesture to the couch. "How about some *Halo*?"

We play through a couple of campaigns, and it's like yesterday never happened—except for his warmth at my side and the high fives that sting my palm most deliciously when we defeat a foe. After a particularly hard-fought battle, I cup his cheek, then brush a gentle, tentative kiss to his lips. "Thank you for not giving up on me."

"I'm a SEAL, angel. We don't give up on anyone."

We're well into our third campaign when West's phone buzzes on the coffee table. He curses as he glances at the screen. "I have to take this. It's my weekend manager."

"Bedroom's back that way." I gesture down the hall. "If you want some privacy."

He shakes his head. After a gruff greeting, West's whole body stills. "How many?" A pause and then he's on his feet, stalking to the open balcony door. "We're not teaching to a fad, Vasquez. And even if we did, the customers we'd gain by converting the locker rooms to a spin theater wouldn't offset the construction costs."

West runs a hand through his hair with a heavy sigh. "I know. See if you can talk Yasmin into giving me another month. Everyone loves her. The rest...I'll figure something out. The Horizon program should generate enough interest to keep us going."

As night bruises the sky and the first stars twinkle over Elliot Bay, West turns back to me. Frustration gathers between his brows and in the set of his shoulders. "I should go. I've got to be at the dojo for the 7:00 a.m. class."

The reluctance edging his tone spurs me into action, and I limp over to him, slide my hands down his arms, and then link our fingers. "What's wrong?"

"People think gyms rake in the dough. Truth is, I'm barely hanging on. People want the latest fitness craze. CrossFit, Spin, Barre, some shit where you pretend you're drumming with these weighted sticks—they call it 'Pound.' There's a new one every year. Krav Maga is different. Fitness is a side benefit. We teach self-defense, how to appreciate your body—no matter its size or shape —honor your abilities and then push through them. Yet I still get a dozen calls a week asking if we offer Pilates or worse—Zumba." He rolls his eyes and lets out a heavy sigh. "We lost three more members this weekend to the new CrossFit place across the street, and one of my best instructors is threatening to quit because she sees her class size dwindling and worries she'll be out of a job soon anyway."

"How bad is it?"

As he stares past me, out over the city, he frowns. "Bad enough that I don't know that we'll be in business next summer. Not without a miracle."

In his moment of vulnerability, I realize what I refused to admit before: we'd moved beyond gaming buddies before ever I set foot in that coffee shop. I care for this man—enough to hurt when he hurts and care that he might lose something so important to him.

I can't help him with his customers or his staff, but I can offer him comfort. Sliding my arms around his neck, I use him for leverage so I can brush my lips against his. His short layer of stubble tickles as he pulls me closer and deepens the kiss. When he presses for more, I yield, my knees going weak as he drops his hands to cup my ass.

Too soon, he breaks off the kiss to stare down at me, his eyes shining with flecks of gold amid the blue. "What happens now?"

All night, I've been pondering that same question, but I didn't have an answer.

Until now. "Sleep is overrated, don't you think?"

With his fingers splayed against my back, he claims my mouth, and rational thought flees. His low rumble of agreement accompanies him sweeping me off my feet, and he carries me into the bedroom as if I weigh nothing at all.

Panic sets in after he deposits me on the bed. I push up on an elbow. "West, I'm—" What? Broken? Scarred? Crippled? He's seen me walk. He knows all of that. The reality of my injuries can't be ignored, but I shake my head as he pulls off his t-shirt, blinded by the sheer beauty of him. Ink covers his chest, down his right arm, his ribs. Names in a flowing script, the SEAL insignia, and lilies decorate his skin, and I want to trace every line. His jeans fall to the floor, leaving him in a pair of tight red briefs that do little to contain his arousal.

"What are you, angel? Smart? Sexy? Gorgeous?" He's next to me before I can answer, brushing the hair away from my neck. Goosebumps prickle along my bare arms as he kisses me again, the heat of him setting me ablaze like I haven't felt in years. "You have me at a disadvantage," he says as he slides his hands under my t-shirt to skim my waist.

"Let no one ever say I don't fight fair." I lift my arms as he tugs my shirt over my head, and the catch of his breath gives me a little thrill when he sweeps a hungry gaze over my black lace bra. Yoga pants quickly follow the t-shirt's path, and I'm already soaked with need.

His hand hovers inches from the worst of the scars along my hip. "I won't hurt you, will I?"

"No."

The rough pads of his fingers scrape against my sides. "You're beautiful, Cam."

"You're blind." Heat rushes to my cheeks—and elsewhere—as he explores my body, teasing kisses along the thin straps of lace at my hips, a lingering touch along my thigh. Then he traps me between his legs so he can stare up at me.

"Tell me about these." He traces the ink on my arm. The birds soar over my bicep amid the pockmarked divots and ridges from the fire and the shrapnel. Ivy winds around my wrist, all the way up to my elbow.

"Therapy," I whisper, so desperate for more I don't want to talk. He won't let me wriggle free, though, and I sag against the firm hold he has on my hips. "Long story."

I've said the wrong thing, and he releases me and leans back on the bed. "I meant what I said earlier." He continues when I raise my brows, "I want to know you." With a quick glance down at his erection, he chuckles. "Yes, I want more than conversation. It's taking every ounce of my self-control not to rip those panties off and ravish you right now. If all I wanted was sex, though, I could get that on Tinder. Or hell, go down to any bar in Pioneer Square on a Friday night.

"You're the first person I've met in a long time I want to truly know. Everything. How do you like your eggs in the morning?"

Laughing, I start to relax. "I'm more of a pancake girl."

"Steak? Rare or medium? Please don't say well done." West leans back as he waits for my answer, and I feign embarrassment. I can't hold the ruse, though. "Medium rare."

"Oh, thank God. I thought we were going to be doomed before we even got started." With my injured wrist held lightly in his hands, he kisses the fingers that haven't felt a damn thing for ten years, accepting a part of me I didn't know needed acceptance. A single tear burns as he continues to caress the ivy, following the vines with his lips.

"I refused to look in the mirror for six months after the bombs. I wore long sleeves and pants every day, even to bed." I clear my throat, trying to stay in the moment. West pulls me on top of him, then kisses his way along my jaw, and I take a steady breath. "My therapist lost a leg in Desert Storm. She'd tattooed her stump with this amazing aquatic design. Said every time she saw herself naked now, she saw the tattoo first, *then* the missing limb. She was right."

45

"Smart woman," he says as he scrapes his teeth along the curve of my neck. "Like that, do you?" he murmurs against my ear as I shiver.

"Uh-huh." I arch my back as he teases a finger under the hem of my lace thong.

"Patience, angel."

West worships me—that's the only word that fits his slow exploration, the way he appreciates every moan, every gasp. By the time I'm naked, dew glistens over my skin, and I'm close to begging. He's taken me to the edge time and time again with his tongue, his teeth, and his fingers.

Lifting his head from between my legs, he licks his lips. "You said something?"

"Bastard," I pant. "You know damn well what I said."

"Something about not stopping?" With that, he nibbles my inner thigh.

I yelp, squirming against his grip.

"Maybe I've teased you enough." He rolls to the side and then fumbles for his pants next to the bed, coming away with a condom that he tosses onto the sheets next to me. If he's not inside me soon, I won't survive, and though I want to take as much time exploring him as he took with me, I don't know that I can. It's been a long time since I had anything but my vibrator for company, and a warm, willing man in my bed who's sculpted like a Greek god has me feeling wanton.

I don't have enough leverage—or enough strength left—to tug off his briefs, but he stills my fumbling fingers as I try. "We'll get to that."

I can't help pouting.

"This is all about you, angel." Despite his words, he yanks off the offending material. No disappointment there, as I think whoever tried to approximate perfection with him came damn close. Short, wiry curls surround his cock, and I palm his length, sliding my hand up and down until he groans, captures my wrist, and pins my arm over my head.

As he returns his attention to my throbbing clit, I writhe against the sheets. Any higher and I'll shoot into the stratosphere without an anchor, but the firm pressure of his hands keeps me grounded, even as I lose all ability to think or breathe. Waves of pleasure buffet me, my entire body dissolving into the roar of my release.

I don't know when he moved, but he's holding me as I come down, and when I kiss him, I taste only me on his lips. Trailing a hand over his chest, I'm amazed this man wasn't snatched up years ago. A jagged scar bisects one of his obliques, another slashes over his shoulder. I trace the SEAL insignia. "What team?"

"Eight." His eyes darken—I've touched a nerve. I try to smooth over my gaffe with another kiss. Soon, his breath quickens, and as I stroke his firm length, I'm rewarded when his eyes flutter closed.

Before I can do much more, he pushes up on an elbow, then tears through the foil packet. "Tell me how I won't hurt you." His voice holds a rough edge.

"Don't ask me that question." I cup the back of his neck to pull him closer. "Just fuck me."

He slides halfway home, accompanied by my gasp. Just as I relax, he pushes deeper, the tenuous hold on his own control evident in the veins pulsing in his neck.

"Oh God, Cam. You're so fucking tight." His first thrust spears me in two, and a lance of pleasure curls my toes. The muscles of his arms cord as he bears himself over me, increasing his pace, and we're both breathing heavily. I can't tear my gaze away from his. He shifts down to one elbow so he can reach between us, and when he finds my sweet spot with a finger, I implode.

A second later, his eyes roll back as he comes, and then he's on top of me, sliding his arms around me so he can hold me close and bury his face in my hair through the aftershocks of our shared climaxes. "I wish I didn't have to leave."

I want to ask him to stay, but he's got an early morning—as do I. Easing back so I can meet his sated gaze, I sigh. "This Coana job is going to take every spare minute of my time this week." I link our fingers. "But what are you doing on Friday night...and Saturday morning?"

"Well, there's this woman I usually play Halo with, but I think she has plans on Friday." He grins and then kisses me so thoroughly, I'm breathless once more. "Maybe she wants company?"

"Hell, yes."

6

CAM

*R*oyce lumbers through the door, a scowl twisting his lips. "You two. My office. Now."

Lucas rolls his eyes when Royce is gone. "Good morning to you too, boss," he mutters so only I can hear.

"He's still in a mood. You don't want to fuck with him." When Royce is like this, you're better off putting your head down and riding it out.

"Guess you didn't get through to him yesterday." Lucas heads into Royce's office, and I sigh.

Whatever's up Royce's ass must be serious, as he's never gone this long in one of his moods. Still, the guy's as loyal as they come, which is the only reason I stay when really, I could write my own ticket with a lot less stress.

Once I've taken a seat next to Lucas, Royce stares us down. "I went over Cam's schedule yesterday afternoon. Given LaCosta's deadline and the amount of work we're going to have to do to get the cameras up and running, I asked Al to find us some help. He's bringing in two guys to start tomorrow."

"Does that mean I can have Lucas back on debugging?"

Lucas swivels his head in my periphery. *Oh shit. Royce didn't tell Lucas he'd have to help with the cabling.*

Royce runs a hand over his jaw, though he doesn't quite manage to cover his scowl. "Al's new. He's run electrical before, and he's got great references, but he doesn't know CAT-5. Not well enough to supervise a job like this on his own. The temp agency needs at least a week's lead time to get me anyone qualified, and Brian's got a week left on his medical leave." With a terse shake of his head, Royce meets Lucas's gaze. "Even with Al bringing in two of his friends with electrical certifications, we're still two men down. I need Lucas to supervise the cabling."

I can't look at Lucas. Focusing on my knees instead, I try to come up with something to ease the sting. It's no use, though. Lucas is so much better than cabling, but he's fast and such a perfectionist that nothing gets by him.

"Cam?" The strain in Lucas's voice tugs at my heart. "You wanted me to start the final customizations today."

"My decision's final," Royce snaps. Someone knocks on the door, and Lucas flinches as I mouth a pitiful apology. Royce stands, bracing a hand on his desk. "Al, come on in."

The man hovering in the doorway smiles as he strips off his jacket. By the look of his brown leather bomber, this summer storm is a doozy. "I hope I'm not interrupting."

"You're not. Al Hagen, meet Camilla Delgado and Lucas Parker. They'll be overseeing your work."

I extend my hand, and Al's firm grip is accompanied by an odd expression. Almost surprise. Then again, most people look twice at my cane when they meet me. "Call me Cam."

"You're the programmer?" Vague disbelief infuses his tone.

I'm used to being looked down on in the tech world. Not only am I a woman, but I'm also Mexican. My brown skin and inky locks don't earn me as much prejudice in Seattle as they would in Fresno or Modesto—where I grew up—but for every five enlightened Seattleites, one is still stuck in the dark ages.

"I am." I plant my cane and push to my feet. Al's stocky but short, and I have a couple of inches on him. *Thank you, Papa, for your height.* "Ever since I left the army."

"Oh. Great." He can't turn away fast enough, and when he gets to Lucas, he offers another handshake. "So…what's the plan?" He addresses Royce, rather than either one of us, and I'm starting to really dislike this guy.

"Cam's the project lead. Lucas is going to oversee the cabling. You'll take your orders from them. Get to work." Royce stands as well, dismissing us, and I can't help the twitch in my right arm. The urge to salute him lingers, even a decade after our last mission together. But I manage to limit myself to a curt nod, and the three of us head for the bullpen.

"Listen," I begin when we're standing at my desk, but before I can give Al a piece of my mind—professionally, of course—he holds up his hand.

"Please. Let me say something first. I really need this job. And I don't want to let anyone down. You tell me what to do, I'll do it. Hell, I'll crawl through the dingiest, darkest ventilation ducts the hotel has just so I can work. And I'm sorry for earlier. I didn't mean to imply a woman can't handle this job. Royce called you 'Cam' when we met the other day, and I thought it was short for Cameron."

He's so earnest, I relent and gesture to the conference room. "Schematics are in there. Get yourself some coffee, and we'll go over the plan."

―――――――

BY MIDDAY, Lucas, Al, and the crew are set up in the parking garage, and I'm headed back to Coana to check on them and install Oversight's base framework. None of her modules are fully customized yet, but what I have to do today will form the foundation of the entire system.

My phone buzzes as I step onto the elevator.

How am I supposed to go all week without seeing you? Will you have time to game tonight?

If my heritage allowed me to blush easily, I'd be crimson right now. I had more than one dream that involved West last night, so I rush to reply.

You'll be begging for mercy, stud.

By the time we've exchanged a few racier texts, I've set up my laptop and hooked into Coana's network. Their existing security feeds reveal Lucas and the crew hard at work. Al and his friends chat amiably, with Lucas off on his own, miserable. I've got to find a way to make things up to him.

The next few hours drag on, though the install goes off without any major hitches. Well past six, as I'm contemplating packing up, I call Lucas up to the server room, hoping I can find a way to cheer him.

"What's up?" He's covered in cobwebs and dust, with a particularly thick smudge under his eye. "We're done for the day. About to head home."

The keycard slides across the narrow desk. "Royce has three interviews scheduled on Thursday. I can't override him—and we won't finish this job without you running cable this week. But consider this a promise. As soon as he hires someone, I'll rely on you here. In this chair."

Lucas spins the card in his palm. "Cam, I...Thank you."

"How's everything going?"

After a shrug, he drops into the chair next to me. "Al's good. Hard worker. His buddies could use some social skills, but they've done what I've asked without complaint. We're going to try to get through the seventh floor by the end of the week."

I glance down at the schedule and smile. "If you can do that, you'll be back in this chair before you know it."

"Did you ever call that guy and apologize? The SEAL?" The coat of Lucas's frustration slides away, and all of a sudden I've got my friend back. "Do I need to steal your phone and take matters into my own hands?"

"Never!" I snatch the phone up and hold it to my chest. "We're having dinner on Friday."

"That's all I get? Spill it, Delgado. I need details."

Before long, we're laughing like there's never been any tension between us, and a piece of my life slips back into place.

WEST

"You ready to admit defeat, frogman?" Cam's laugh carries over the speakers, and I pull a couple of advanced combo skills out of my bag of tricks, sending her avatar tumbling off the edge of the spinning satellite.

"Never." Her character respawns, and as we wait for the game to take us back to the save point, I trace a finger through the condensation gathering on my water glass. "You've been quiet tonight, angel. Bad day at work?"

Her sigh carries over the line. "The client moved up the schedule, and we're all scrambling. Royce assigned Lucas to cabling, so all of the code's on me now. I can handle it, but I know Lucas is upset."

"How'd you two meet?" For six weeks, we've talked and laughed and joked every day, but Cam's often danced around her past. Now that we're...more...I want to know everything about her, tell her everything about me—even the dark, painful pieces that haunt my nightmares.

She snorts, such a delicate and irreverent sound, and I'm so mesmerized that I don't realize her character's taken off running. "When I first moved to Seattle, I lived in this tiny studio apartment on Capitol Hill. I'd left rehab—well before they wanted me to— and I was on crutches."

Her voice softens, a bit of nostalgia creeping in, and I pause the game. "Angel, turn on your webcam."

53

After a long minute, her picture pops up on the screen, and she smiles shyly at me. "I'm a mess."

"You're gorgeous. So, you're on crutches…"

She runs a hand through her hair, and I wish I could feel the silky strands over my own fingers. "I was going stir crazy stuck in my apartment. The Egyptian Theater had a showing of *Enemy of the State*—remember that one?—and I trekked through the rain, four blocks, on crutches, to get there. I'm soaked to the bone, everything hurts, and I probably looked like a drowned rat. A few seats away, this big guy starts shaking his head and muttering at the screen whenever they get the tech wrong in the film."

I raise a brow. "And you didn't poke him with one of your crutches so he'd shut up?"

She laughs. "I thought about it, but he was right about every scene. As the credits rolled, I leaned over and said, 'Don't you hate it when bad tech ruins a good movie?'"

"You should never watch reruns of *CSI: Cyber*."

"I saw the first episode and almost lost my voice yelling at the television." Cam shakes her head. "Lucas and I criticized the movie's computer scenes the whole way out of the theater and down the block. We probably would have gone our separate ways, but then it started to hail. We ducked into a pizza place and ended up talking for two hours. I admit I was a little disappointed to learn he was gay.

"The storm passed, and he walked me back to my apartment building. I stopped at the door, stared at him, and said, 'Aren't you going to say something?'" Cam jams her hand on her hip in an exaggerated motion. "'Say something about what, hon?' he asked. When I gestured towards my crutches, he just looked baffled. 'Your terrible taste in rain coats? Because, damn. You need something better than that to survive in this town.'" She looks down and whispers the next words with so much emotion that I ache to wrap my arms around her. "I hated myself back then. Hated what I looked like, hated that my injuries were the first thing everyone saw. Everyone but Lucas." When she looks up again, she's almost beaming. "After that day, we saw a movie every Sunday afternoon for almost a year."

"He sounds like a good guy."

"He is. You'll like him."

Knowing she wants me to meet her friends soothes the raw frustration of spending half the day with my accountant, and as we launch another campaign, I can't help but wonder how I'll make it to Friday without kissing her again.

CAM

Back in the office the next day, I try to ignore Royce's closed door in favor of working out some of Oversight's bugs. The longer I sit at my desk, though, the harder this becomes. When Royce stalks out of his office and heads for the lounge, I roll my eyes at Orion, our mobile developer.

"Say something," Orion whispers. "He'll listen to you."

I'm not so sure about that, but I have to try, for all of our sakes. This gruff, pissy Royce isn't helping anyone, and with ZoomWare coming up, and the Coana job on such a tight schedule, despite Lucas's excellent job finishing the second floor in a single day, we need our "fearless leader."

Off I go, and I can't help hearing "The Imperial March" as I shuffle into the lounge to find Royce slumped in the bean bag chair, playing *Grand Theft Auto* with the sound down.

We're all geeks. Even Royce—sort of. Gaming is the one thing everyone in the office can agree on.

"You okay?"

He looks up, swears under his breath, and pauses the game. "Can't a guy decompress in peace?"

"Whoa. You want to be alone, you be alone." I wish I could stalk, but all I can manage is a slow lope back to my desk. Nothing I do today is working, from Oversight's cataloging module to talking to the man who used to be my surrogate big brother. It's a damn good thing I'm not planning on seeing West tonight, or I'd find some way to screw that up, too.

I wrestle with the code for another two hours, unable to figure out why every time I compile, the whole system crashes. The software has been stable for months. All I'm doing now is making the tweaks we'll need to make for every customer: file storage locations, employee accounts, and some of the optional bits, like HVAC controls and emergency lighting overrides. Around me, the office stills as one person, and then another, and another heads home. Soon, Royce and I are the only two left, and he's back in his office with the door closed.

As I'm packing up, he pokes his head out. "Can I talk to you?"

I manage to contain my scowl, but it's touch-and-go there for a moment. "If you're not going to jump down my throat, sure."

His expression goes from unsure to pained as he steps aside so I can pass. "I deserved that."

I steel myself as I shut the door behind me.

"I need you to handle the interviews on Thursday." Royce collapses back into his chair, and before his words sink in, I think I see a wince deepen the lines around his eyes. My anger flares, along with a thread of concern.

"And when am I supposed to *finish the damn code?* You kept the specs from us for too long, and now you can't even hire the help we might not have needed if you'd *been here?*"

"Look, I know I fucked up—"

"Royce, you need to tell me what's going on." I jerk my head back towards the bullpen. "You've got a team of people out there who'd move virtual mountains for you—all because you gave them a chance. And—" I can't stop myself, but my voice fades to a whisper. "—you've got me."

Royce slams his hand down on his desk before I finish speaking. Pens jump, and a stress ball topples onto the floor. Rather fitting. "I'm trying to fix things!"

"You're doing a piss poor job of it." I take a step closer, but something in his expression stops me. His gaze hardens, and the reinforced steel wall between us gains another layer. Blinking quickly, I try to stop the burning tear that threatens.

"Jesus, Cam. I'm sorry, okay?"

"No." Through sheer force of will, I keep the tremor from my voice. "I'm exhausted. I'm working twelve hour days on this project. With Lucas overseeing the hardware, I'm stretched thin. I don't need your attitude on top of everything."

I turn to leave, fed up with this conversation and with Royce. But he rounds his desk and touches my arm. "Cam, I know I haven't been the easiest person to work with lately. Running this company...I love what I do, but the pressure can be intense." He frowns, the lines around his eyes deepening with the motion. "Diffusing bombs didn't leave me this fucked at the end of the day. Juggling projects, paying the bills, hustling for new clients...everything I do is to protect this team. Everything. I'm sorry for snapping at you earlier. It won't happen again. I'll get Abby to handle the interviews."

We haven't been this close in ten years—he smells like the cloves from his cigarettes. His apology hangs in the space between us, and as I search his gaze, I wonder what, exactly, he's apologizing for.

Say something. Anything. Honest conversation isn't our strong suit anymore, and I chicken out, giving his forearm a squeeze. "Get some rest, Royce. Cut the staff some slack. Maybe bring in doughnuts tomorrow.

"We won't let you down. This job? ZoomWare? We want Emerald City to succeed as much as you do. You just have to trust us a little more." If I stay a minute longer, I'll say something I regret, so I slip out of the office, and I think I hear him whisper, "I'll try."

7

WEST

*W*ith his head bowed so his black hair hangs over his eyes, the sullen kid across from me fidgets. Picking at his Mariner's t-shirt, scratching an itch that can't be there on his prosthetic forearm, and occasionally glancing over to the mats to watch the afternoon advanced class going through their moves, he's obviously trying to play it cool in front of his mom.

"How safe is it?" His mother leans forward and drops her voice. As if the kid can't hear from a foot away.

"Very." I pass her a handout. "All four instructors, including me, have been through extensive training with the country's best rehabilitation specialists. Jack Maneli is based out of Seattle Children's Hospital, and he's—"

"Manny?" The kid's interest piqued, he shoves his swath of greasy hair away from his brown eyes.

I try to hide my chuckle. Jack "Manny" Maneli has a reputation for being the coolest physical therapist in Seattle, and his work with young amputees has put him on the map. "Yep. Manny trained me personally. Said I wasn't in bad shape. Then he made me fight him. I lost."

The kid's eyes widen. "Mom, please."

"Will there be a doctor on site?"

"Manny's going to attend the first class, and after that, we'll have one of his interns at every session. As part of the certification process, all of our instructors go through extensive CPR, injury assessment, and emergency response lessons that we repeat every four years."

Uncertainty swims in the woman's eyes, but when she glances down at her son, who now sits up straight with a grin spreading across lips I bet usually wear a permanent frown, she nods. "Okay. Where do we sign up?"

FOR THE FIFTH time in half an hour, I try to loosen my tie. The young man across the desk from me, who probably graduated college last year, enters all of my information into the bank's computer. "Just a few more minutes, Mr. Sampson."

Everything I've worked for comes down to a computer algorithm. Yes or no. A good candidate for a loan or a poor one. A business with potential or one that'll be gone within the year. How can a computer answer those questions when I can't?

I see the faces of the eighteen kids waiting to start the new Horizon program. The hope in their parents' eyes convinced me this is the right thing to do. Hell, I've got a dozen men and women from VetNet ready to sign up for classes—if I can afford the goddamn insurance.

The computer beeps, and my hope fades in an instant.

"You have excellent credit, Mr. Sampson. But with the decline in your income over the past six months, Sound Trust can't extend a loan to you at this time. We do offer a credit card with a ten-thousand-dollar cash advance and an annual percentage rate of twenty-nine-point-seven percent." He ends his spiel with a smile, and it takes everything I have not to snatch the file folder from his hands and introduce him to some of the more colorful phrases I learned in the navy.

"No, thank you." The words struggle to escape through gritted teeth. "Can I talk to your manager? Plead my case? I know my membership numbers haven't been the greatest lately, but the Horizon program will attract an entirely new set of customers—one that can't find the classes they need anywhere else."

Sympathy swims in the young man's gaze. "The computer's decision is final, sir. I'm very sorry."

GARRETT SLIDES the frosty pint glass across the bar. "On the house. You look like someone stole your puppy."

"Another day, another bank telling me I'm not worth the risk." The icy lager soothes my raw nerves. "They'll let me take out a cash advance on a credit card, though."

"Let me guess? Thirty percent interest?" He shakes his head. "Fuckers. By the time I got the money to buy this place, a couple of the bank managers knew me on sight."

"How'd you finally pull it off?" Though half of Libations' tables sit empty, most of the locals aren't off work yet. By 7:00 p.m., the hostess will have to turn people away.

With a dry laugh, Garrett slams a glass down on a cocktail shaker. "I came up with half of the down payment on my own. Saved every fucking penny. Stopped going out, ate ramen a couple times a week, taught a few craft cocktail classes for the local grocery co-op, took odd jobs whenever I could."

Ryker's visit still weighs on me. "One of the guys I...*helped*... get out of Afghanistan offered me a job last week. Five large for a few days' work."

Garrett whistles. "What's the problem, then?" He sets the drink on a tray for one of his servers, then leans a hip against the back

61

wall and rubs his thigh. Most people would never guess that he lost a leg in Afghanistan, but on his bad days, the limp is obvious.

"It's K&R work on foreign soil. High value targets, high risk. That's not my world anymore." Even as I finish the sentence, I know I don't have a choice. Two jobs and I'd have enough to pay for the insurance on the Horizon program for kids *and* for adults. Half a dozen missions and I could open in a new location far away from that fucking CrossFit studio.

"Listen," Garret says as he braces his hands on the bar. "If I'd had the chance—and the ability—to make that kind of money that fast before I got the loan for Libations, I would have jumped at it."

"Hey, stranger!" Lilah, Garrett's fiancé, lays a delicate hand on my shoulder as she leans in to kiss my cheek. "Where've you been? We haven't seen you since the engagement party."

"Playing a lot of *Halo*."

"Huh?" She yelps then laughs as Garrett swoops in from behind her, grabs her around the waist, and spins her before capturing her lips in a searing kiss.

"Explain," she says once she's seated next to me with a Long Wet Kiss—the drink Garrett invented for her long before they fell in love. "What's Halo? Or...*who's* Halo?"

"*Halo's* an Xbox game. Though I did meet someone." Longing stirs inside me as memories of Cam laughing, Cam sipping espresso, Cam naked and moaning rise to the surface.

Lilah quirks a brow and waits for me to explain.

"Cam is..." As I try to come up with words worthy of Cam, Garrett twines his fingers with Lilah's across the bar for just a moment before he starts on another drink order. The tender gesture is probably an unconscious one on his part, and their love shines brighter than the spotlights on the multi-colored bottles that line the bar. "Lilah, hang on a sec." I lean forward. "Garrett, would you take that job now?"

He meets my gaze, a bottle of bourbon held aloft. "No. Not a chance."

CAM

As I dig into my chicken piccata, I replay the day's events, and anger and frustration simmer. Sure, Royce apologized. But he didn't *say* anything. Not really.

What's worse? I let him get away with it.

Sometimes I think I'm more of a coward than he is. He opened the door. Why didn't I take that time to push—delicately—about his mood the past few weeks? Or all the other crap between us that's been unsaid for so long?

Answer: because I might have lost him completely. And I'm afraid that would break me, yet again.

At least West is waiting for me, and once I sign in to Xbox Live and take my first sip of wine, I relax. "Ready to submit to my superior alien-fighting prowess?"

West chuckles. "Bring it, angel."

"Oh, you'll regret that. I've had a shitty day, and I'm ready to take my frustrations out on your Spartan." I cut down his character with my first shot. "You'll be begging for mercy by the end of the night."

"What happened today?"

A volley sails toward my soldier, and I roll to the side, then come up firing. Another hit, another curse, and we're set upon by a horde of aliens. "The Coana job is getting to me." I fill him in on today's events as I decimate another group of hostiles, and when I've secured a tidy victory, I drop the controller in my lap and close my eyes. "Do you ever feel like it's you against the world?"

Silence greets me, and I wrack my brain for something light, fun, easy. Desperate to fill the void between us, I pick up my controller, but he saves me from my awkwardness before I can respawn my character.

"All the time. Ten people depend on me for their paychecks. And when things go wrong, I have no one to blame but myself."

His voice roughens. "I've got a great team. But at the end of the day, my ass is on the line for every decision I make. The pressure never lets up."

"How do you handle it?"

His strained laugh belies his easy words. "I take my frustrations out on the punching bag or one of my sparring partners. Blow shit up with you at night."

"Did you convince your instructor to stay?"

"For a while." He doesn't elaborate, and I don't push. Soon, we're back to shooting aliens on screen and talking about movies. Well, I'm talking. He's mostly giving me one- or two-word answers. By the end of the night, I feel worse than when we started.

"You're upset. Talk to me."

A heavy sigh carries over the line. "I want to launch this new program. No one else offers anything like it outside of New York City and Los Angeles. Once I get it off the ground, the CrossFit place becomes just a blip on the radar. But if I can't get a loan for the extra insurance costs, though, it's dead in the water. The bank didn't look kindly at my books today."

"Oh. I'm sorry, West."

Ice clinks in a glass. "I've had to take on some private security work. Rent-a-cop shit. I won't be around tomorrow night. Some corporate party where the CEO 'only wants the best.' It's at a country club for fuck's sake. The most excitement I'm going to see is an entitled board member puking on the golf course."

More ice rattles and his voice takes on a very different tone. Deeper. Guttural. Sensual. "If I call you when I get home...will you tell me what you're wearing?"

BEFORE I HEAD FOR BED, I pop on VetNet. I've been neglecting them, and though we both fought sleep for as long as we could, West lost the battle and started snoring over his headset a few minutes ago. I'm still wired, so I start a new thread, hoping for some levity.

The meds are kicking in, and I'm a little loopy. Anyone got a funny story to share? I'll start. I'm working this killer job right now. Long hours. I order a grilled cheese and fries for lunch today on my way back from the client, and when the waiter delivers the meal, he trips over my laptop bag. The sandwich flies apart, both pieces of bread landing cheese side down on the floor, and fries pelt me. One fell down my shirt and settled in my bra. No big deal, accidents happen. But three hours later, when I'm meeting with my boss, he finds a French fry in my hair.

I should really shower. I think there's still French fry grease between my breasts. Royce looked so uncomfortable fishing the fry out of my dark locks, but to his credit, he said nothing. Just tossed the offending shoestring into the trash.

Soon, the thread is full of replies. Everything from poorly-fitting prosthetics falling off in the middle of sex to walking in on coworkers kissing in the supply closet to attending a client meeting with an open fly or a pair of panties clinging to a sweater. I'm laughing so hard tears are threatening, and the bone-deep ache in my hip has faded to an uncomfortable burn.

Relaxed now, I take a few minutes to poke around some of the other threads, commiserating with LT4Life on the Chronic Pain board, sending BlueBayone a list of good physical therapists in Tacoma, and posting cute baby animal pics on the Light and Fluffy board. Hey, everyone needs a baby panda now and again.

Over on the Vents and Rants board, HuskyFan has a new post.

We got the bill for our temporary insurance today. We don't have enough money in the bank. My new job pays well—for what it is—but not well enough. Even if I cancel my own coverage and just take care of my wife and the boy, I don't know that we'll make it. I had to take on some work for a buddy on the side. I'm already working overtime at the day job, and now I need to work nights as well. I'm not sleeping, and my son started crying when I left for work today. Someone tell me it'll be worth it in the end?

I can't reassure him—not the way he needs—but I send him a

private message, hoping that maybe taking his mind off his troubles will help.

FlashPoint: *Hey. I thought you'd like to know that I patched things up with first-date guy. We're seeing each other again on Friday night. I haven't been this excited about someone in a long time.*

A few minutes later, he replies.

HuskyFan: *Tell me about him. Distract me. I'm killing time at the second job waiting for someone else, and it's hard not to wallow.*

For the next half an hour, we trade messages, and though I don't kiss and tell—much—dishing a little about West with a semi-anonymous stranger helps me process why I feel the way I do, even though the relationship is still new. West and I share experiences, despite serving in two different branches of the military. That common thread runs through our lives, and so when West talks about letting his employees down, I don't see just a business owner, but a commanding officer. And when I talk about all the extra work I'm doing to launch Oversight on time, he doesn't see dedication. He sees me taking command of my own team, doing my best under orders from on high. He listens, and asks questions, and when we talk, I feel like he truly understands me.

When HuskyFan fails to respond to my last message, I send him some final words of encouragement before signing off.

FlashPoint: *I hope things get better for you, HF. I'll check in with you in a few days. Don't give up. When I got blown up, I thought my life was over. But now, even on the days the pain's the worst, I'm happy. You'll get there too.*

8

CAM

I'd like to take this day and shove it up Lucas's ass. Dude bailed this morning, leaving Al and the rest of the crew scrambling. Now I'm on the fifth floor, trying to make sense of Lucas's shorthand.

"We'll manage, ma'am." Al takes the notes from me, squints, and shrugs. "The first few days were rough, but everyone knows their shit—um, sorry—stuff now, and we can make up the time."

"You can drop the 'ma'am.' We're all in this together. Camilla or Cam is fine. Lucas says you're doing great work. All of you. But we can't afford any screw-ups on this job."

Al rubs the back of his neck and then nods his head towards the stairwell door. As my footfalls echo on the metal landing, he instructs the rest of the crew to pack up their gear and head up to six. I pull out my phone and read Lucas's message again.

I can't come in until one. Something came up. I'm sorry. I'll work late, but the crew's going to have to fly solo for a while. Sorry.

"Something came up? That something better be damned important," I mutter as I try texting him again. He knows how vital this job is, how much pressure we're under. His voice mail picks up on the second ring, and as I disconnect, I growl, "I'm going to beat you over the head with my cane, Luc." When Al joins me, I'm vibrating with anger—or perhaps that's the extra coffee I ingested to get going today. Unlike Lucas, I managed to show up on only three hours of broken sleep. If I keep stopping at Broadcast every morning, though, I'm going to have to cut some other expense from my budget. Grocery store beans don't compare in taste or price.

"Camilla?" Al's stopped two feet away, and he's eying me like one would a feral animal. My snarl probably doesn't help. "Are you all right?"

"Sorry. I didn't get a lot of sleep last night, and I have to spend the whole day debugging. Go on." I lean against the railing to try to appear less threatening.

He runs a hand through his short-cropped hair. "I sent the rest of the crew up to six to start the prep work there. I didn't want to say anything in front of the guys, but a couple of them made some stupid mistakes the first few floors. Lucas has been working his ass off to try and repair everything, but at this point, we're going to be running right up against the deadline."

The tenuous hold I have on my sanity threatens to slip. "Lucas hasn't said anything." Failing to keep the frustration and hurt from my voice, I force a deep breath and squeeze my eyes shut for a moment. When I'm no longer in danger of launching into an unprofessional tirade, I straighten and meet Al's gaze. "What can I do to help?"

He shifts from one foot to the other as he appears to wrestle with his next words. "If you can get us permission to be here after hours and some overtime pay, my guys and I can work the weekend and try to catch up."

"Done. I'll take care of it today. We've got another eleven days before we have to start live testing, and fourteen floors to go. Anything you need—*anything*—you let me know. Abby's interviewing another three potential electricians today, so hopefully you'll have help by next week."

"Will do. I'll tell the guys." Al pauses at the door and glances back at me. "Are you sure Royce won't mind the overtime?"

I stifle a laugh. "Oh, he'll mind." As Al flinches, I wave my hand. "Leave Royce to me. He might not want to spend the extra money, but he needs this job to go off without a hitch. You just concentrate on getting the job done, and I'll take care of getting you and your guys paid."

He smiles as he nods. "Thank you."

<hr>

By LUNCHTIME, Al's confirmed that he and two of his crew—Zach and Lloyd, I think—will join him tomorrow and Sunday, and I've upgraded their security badges to give them weekend access to the hotel's employee-only areas. I'm avoiding the office—and Royce—by stopping for lunch at Mazie's. Cowardly, I know, but I need a loaded bacon burger to get me through this day. My phone buzzes on the table as I take my first bite, and distracted, I don't notice a glob of Mazie's special sauce fall from my burger and land on my red tank.

"Dammit," I manage through a mouthful of deliciousness. Now I'm going to have to go home and change before I go back to Coana. No way can I show up with a grease stain right over my breast. Hell, I shouldn't even go into the office looking like this, but I can't delay talking to Royce much longer.

After going through four napkins, I check my phone, and my cheeks flame.

I want to slide my fingers into your hair, press you against the wall, and kiss you until you're dripping for me. Then strip you naked so I can taste you, finally taking you over the edge as you scream my name. You've been in my dreams every night, and tomorrow night you're mine.

My fingers shake a little as I type out my reply. He's not the only one who's had intense dreams this week, and I might have packed my overnight bag two days ago, giddy with anticipation—or perhaps arousal.

What if I have a different plan? Like your naked body under me as I kiss every one of your tats, then take you deep and use my tongue in ways you'll dream about for weeks.

I cringe as I send the message. Sex, I'm good at. Actual sexting? Flirting? Not so much. As I finish my last french fry, he replies with a few well-placed *fucks* and dirty promises, though, so I must have done all right. Feeling a little lighter than when I sat down, I head to my car. As I'm fishing for my keys, two men emerge from a high-end Italian restaurant across the street. My purse slips from my arm as I watch Lucas—dressed in a suit—shake hands with a man I recognize from the latest *Seattle TechWorld* issue. They're too far away for me to hear their conversation, but Lucas's tamed dreads, the leather portfolio tucked under his arm, and the hand-shake can only mean one thing.

As Raymond Hawthorne, Head of Development at TechLock, walks away, I regain a measure of composure and snatch up my purse. "Lucas!" I wish I could run across the street, but at my speed, I'd probably get hit by a car. Though that might be prefer-able to this next conversation.

He cringes as he hears me, looks after Hawthorne briefly, then jogs over to me, loosening his tie as he steps onto the sidewalk. "What are you doing here?"

"Having lunch. You want to explain what you were doing with Hawthorne?" I brace a hand against my car door and glare.

Lucas's shoulders slump, and he fiddles with the edge of his portfolio. "Don't tell Royce. Please."

Despite my anger, I keep my voice low. "I have to. You bailed on me, and we're already behind schedule at Coana. Al and his crew are going to have to work the weekend, Oversight crashes every time I try to run a systems test, and we're less than two weeks away from turning her on and running through live drills." I take a deep breath and swallow hard. "Why didn't you tell me?"

His entire body deflates, and he retreats a step, almost cringing.

"I'm a good programmer. Hell, I'm better than good—I could lead a team." Lucas shoves the tie into his jacket pocket. "But I'm never going to do that while you're around. Not that I should—I learned from the best. But I want more than always being in your shadow."

The lump in my throat threatens to choke me, and I look away so I don't have to see the discomfort hunching Lucas's shoulders. "I can't finish this project without you, Luc."

He touches my arm. "I wouldn't leave in the middle of this install. Royce—and you—took a chance on me when no one else would." As I meet his gaze, his voice cracks. "I don't even know if they'll offer me the job. You know my history. Even scoring an interview was a long shot."

Though anger still simmers beneath the surface, he's my best friend, and I can't stand to see him so insecure. "There's no way they'll let you slip through their fingers. You're better than you realize. The functions you wrote for me two weeks ago were the best you've ever done. Maybe better than mine."

"Even if that were true…" He scuffs his shiny black dress shoe on the sidewalk and then takes my hand. His warm fingers tighten on mine, and he holds my gaze, pleading. "Don't say anything to Royce. Not yet. Give me until Monday."

I've never been a very good liar. My mother always said I wore my emotions all over my face. "I've got to tell him something. I need Al and his guys to work the weekend—you too, by the way. We're in danger of blowing the whole damn thing because of LaCosta's stupid party. How am I supposed to spin this so Royce doesn't blow a gasket?"

"Tell him I got food poisoning or something." Lucas raises his brows, hope smoothing the tiny lines around his lips and eyes. "Please, Cam."

"You ate some bad shrimp last night, understand?" When he nods, I continue, "Change out of that suit and get your ass to Coana." I pull away, then dig into my bag for my keys. "And look appropriately nauseous."

Lucas watches me as I drop awkwardly into the driver's seat. "I'm sorry. I should have told you about the interview."

"Yes. You should have." Before I can dwell any longer, I shut the door, leaving Lucas to watch as I pull into traffic.

ONLY THE QUIET click of keys breaks up the silence of the office. If there's one constant among programmers, it's that we like our routines, which means Abby's listening to Enya, and 90s grunge music leaks out of Shemar's headphones. Orion hates music, but blasts white noise at an unhealthy decibel level. Me, I prefer Tibetan Bowls when I'm stressed, Pandora's greatest hits when I'm not. Guess what I'll be listening to this afternoon?

After I dump my bag, I rap on the door to Royce's office.

"Come in." His gruff voice scrapes like broken glass over my nerves, and I take a deep breath before I twist the knob. He doesn't look up as I enter, which affords me a moment to gawk.

Dark circles swell under his eyes, and his hair sticks up on the sides as if he's grabbed the short strands and pulled more than once. Takeout containers overflow the trash can, and the whole room smells like stale coffee. When he drags himself from whatever he's working on, he nods. "Shut the door and tell me what's going on at Coana."

I sink into his guest chair, then pull out my iPad. "We're running behind schedule on cabling. On the software side, I've installed the framework, but the core modules are still buggy."

Royce frowns. "I thought we had this under control. I brought in additional help. Abby had me extend offers to two of the electricians this morning. What the hell is going on over there?"

You mean besides Lucas looking for another job and bailing on me this morning? Clenching my jaw so I don't blurt out Lucas's secret, I search for kernels of truth to offer. "We've discovered a dozen blind spots that we didn't plan on, three employee-only areas that need upgraded biometrics, and the extra cameras we had to order won't arrive until Monday."

"You're not telling me something." He narrows his eyes at me. Biggest disadvantage to working for your former CO? You can't hide a damn thing.

"Lucas called in sick this morning. He's faster than any of the rest of the cabling crew, including Al. Put us at least another half day behind, maybe more."

"What the fuck? He'd better be on his death bed." Royce slams his fist against the desk, rattling his cup full of pens. "Until this job is done, everyone works unless they're bleeding from the eyes. Hang on. I want to talk to him. Right now." He wrenches the receiver from his desk phone, and the momentum sends the base crashing to the floor. "Goddammit!"

If the universe wanted me on Lucas's side, this is all they had to do. No one talks to my team that way, and I'm not Royce's punching bag. "He got food poisoning, Royce." The lie rolls off my tongue, but the bitter flavor turns my stomach. "Did you really want him running cable while puking his guts out? No one needs to see that. Or hear, smell…"

Once he's righted his phone and retrieved the sizable shard of plastic that broke off from the side, he scrubs his hands over his face. "Fine. But he better be back tomorrow."

"He's headed over to the hotel now. I talked to Al, and he offered to work the weekend—thinks he can pull in two of his guys to join him as well. Won't put us completely back on schedule, but we'll be close. I just need you to authorize the overtime." I clench my hands in my lap, hoping Royce agrees and I can escape quickly to go back to my problematic code. At least when Oversight's difficult, she doesn't damage the office equipment.

"Fine." He pushes to his feet, then starts to pace as I blow out a breath. "I don't care what we have to do." Desperation tinges his words, and he rakes a hand through his hair, tugging at the brown strands as he stares at the ceiling. "I met with ZoomWare today. If LaCosta gives us the endorsement he's promised, we have to be

73

ready to turn on Oversight for all of ZoomWare's offices in ninety days. And they want the facial recognition system, too."

I go in for a high-five, but Royce shakes his head, and I flop back into my chair. Why isn't he celebrating? No one has a facial recognition system like we do. This should make him happy.

He grabs his own iPad. "We're going to be on another tight schedule for this one. You're lead. I'm giving you Lucas, Orion, and Abby for this. If you think we need to hire, I'll advertise. Shemar's on the consumer app for the next month, and then he's yours, too."

How am I supposed to handle a contract the size of ZoomWare without Lucas? He knows the code, how I like to work, and all of Oversight's secrets. Breaking in another junior programmer is going to take weeks, if not months. Abby and Orion are fantastic, but they're only partway through their Python certifications, and Shemar hasn't even started. My palms dampen, and I fiddle with the hem of my blouse.

"Cam?" Royce inches forward. "You okay?"

"Y-yeah. Sorry. Just trying to wrap my head around a project this size. If Coana's happy, when would we have to start on their next property?" What's that old cliché? When it rains...

"Let me worry about that. You tell me what you need to get facial recognition working perfectly."

"Another programmer." If Lucas leaves—and that haunted look in his eyes assured me he will before long—I won't have the time to hire when this project is done. I need to get someone else in here now. "Al's shown some pretty strong skills as a project manager. Lucas has been impressed. I could use his help, too."

"Al doesn't want—" Royce rolls his eyes. "He's sticking with cabling. Apprentice-level work only. His choice."

I stifle my sputter, but Royce glares at me anyway.

"You asked me what I needed. Get me someone with at least Lucas's skill set, have Abby and Orion finish their certifications as soon as possible, and find me someone to help with project management."

"Done. That'll be enough?" Royce taps his notes without looking at me, and for the second time in a week, I think I see a tremble in his fingers.

"Yes." Digging for some courage, I stand so we're on equal footing. "There's one more thing." I wave my hand towards the rest of the office. "You've built a great company, Royce. We all love what we do, and until a few weeks ago, we all loved coming into work. Every one of us would move heaven and earth for you."

He stills, and a muscle in his jaw twitches. I rush to continue before he tells me to get the hell out and "leave it alone" again. "We're about to get very busy for a very long time. Everyone needs to be at the top of their game. Including you. Something's changed. You're slamming doors, jumping down people's throats. You broke your phone, for fuck's sake. How long do you think they'll all stick around in this sort of environment? We're too close to 'making it.' Don't screw this up now."

"Screw this up? I'm working my ass off to keep this company together so we can *make it.* What the hell am I supposed to do? Bring puppies and kittens into the office for playtime?" He's straightened, and the fire behind his gaze almost makes me retreat, but I've done that too often with Royce, and now we're both suffering.

"No. Bring back 'Beer Fridays,' buy doughnuts once in a while, suggest we all hit up a happy hour after work—and then *show up.* Anything to let them know you care."

He cringes, looks down at his feet, and then shakes his head. "I care."

"I know that. But I'm not sure they do." I jerk my chin towards the door. "All they see is a boss who's losing control of his demons." I reach out and touch his forearm, hoping he doesn't pull away. "Takes one to know one, Rolls."

"My demons are right where they've always been. If I'm a little short, it's just the stress over this project."

"Royce, this isn't the Coana job. You need help. Are you even sleeping?" His bloodshot eyes hold the answer. "Talk to me. Get on

VetNet. Or see a professional. I could give you the name of my shrink." The hard muscles of his forearm shift under my fingers. "I would have died for you in Afghanistan. You know that, right?"

He jerks away. "You almost did."

"No. I almost died because some Taliban asshole wanted to take out an entire convoy. That's not my point. You're important to me. As is this company. I won't let it—or you—go down without a fight." I reach over and grab a pen and Post-It from his desk. "Here's my therapist's name. Go talk to her. Or…talk to someone. And try to go easy on the rest of them, okay?"

As I press the note into his hand, he tightens his grip, holds onto me for a breath, and then releases me and turns away. Without another word, I slip out of his office and head back to work hoping that this time, he'll listen.

BY THE TIME I sink into my recliner later that night, Royce has sent a company-wide email asking everyone to happy hour the next day. I can't refuse—not after my plea in his office—even though I've been looking forward to my date with West all week. I send a suggestive text, then follow it up with another asking for a favor. Maybe if we engage in a little sexting after his job tonight…or at least heavy flirting…he'll forgive me for rescheduling.

Too tired to go back to my buggy code, I check out the latest threads on VetNet.

Three new members joined us this week, and I welcome them, share a few of my tips for dealing with well-meaning, but dense, family members, and let them know what they'll find on the resources boards. The Amputee board has a dozen unread posts, mostly WonderLT talking about his physical therapy, and the Vents and Rants board has been quiet, except for HuskyFan.

HuskyFan: *I've earned enough from my side job to pay the hospital bills, but I don't have enough cushion to cover the insurance premiums. I can't do this alone, and if I ask for help, I could end up in an even bigger* hole. *Every time my wife looks at me, I see the disappointment in her eyes. My son doesn't understand why Mommy can't get out of bed, and my mother-in-law won't even speak to me. Though that's probably for the best. One mistake and my whole life goes to shit. I can't let things go on like this. I have to get flush again. You're the only ones who understand. Why did I let my brother talk me into enlisting? I could have gotten a job and used my skills to kick some serious ass. I'd be a CEO now. Hell, I could be giving Bill Gates a run for his money. Instead, I come home covered in dirt and cobwebs, and the only time I get to use my skills is working a side job for someone I hate. Why can't I get ahead?*

His agony bleeds through his words. I spent years after my injuries beating myself up for running into the arms of Uncle Sam, but after enough therapy, I realized no amount of misery would change the past. I drain the last of my lemonade and type out a quick reply.

FlashPoint: *You're not alone. If I'd known I'd get blown up, I'd have gladly begged my family to take me back. But at the time, joining the army was a lot more attractive. All we can do is make the best of what we have now. Your wife and son and the baby-on-the-way should be your main concerns. Ignore your mother-in-law as best you can, and tell your wife how much you love her and how committed you are to finding a solution. And if you haven't, find a professional to talk to. My shrink saved my life. More than once.*

Half an hour later, I take a break from the card key module to find a reply.

HuskyFan: *Thanks, but my jobs are eating up every spare minute. I'm checking in from my side job, and I won't be able to go home for another three or four hours. Once things calm down and the baby's born, I'll look at that list you sent me. But, if you don't mind me asking, what happened with your family?*

I'm not ready to answer that question. Even fourteen years later, the pain of that day can send me into my own private hell, clutching my grandmother's letter—the one with the only photos I have left of my family—as the burn of tear-brined bourbon masks the overwhelming guilt at my cowardice. But I can't ignore him.

That won't help either of us. With one last look at the bottle I keep on my kitchen counter, I shove the memories away—back to the dark recesses of my mind where they can't hurt me tonight.

FlashPoint: *I was a stupid kid. The details aren't important, but I ran off to the army to try to fix what I broke. Don't make my mistakes. Put your family first. You can do that by taking care of yourself. I know it probably feels like you don't have time to see a shrink right now, but trust me—make the time.*

HuskyFan: *Did it work? Running away?*

FlashPoint: *No. I don't think it ever does.*

I log off, unwilling to relive those dark days for anyone, and return to Oversight. My eyes water. Well after midnight, I run system diagnostics on the card reader module and the error rate skyrockets. Again.

"Come on, baby. Talk to me." After another hour, I've debugged another module, but West hasn't called. As I fall into bed, the meds turning the world fuzzy and warm, I hope he's okay and that HuskyFan finds some peace.

9

WEST

*T*he squawk in my ear might as well be a whisper for all I react. Training I'd thought long forgotten races back in a heartbeat as another member of the security team offers the "all clear" from the parking lot.

From my post at the south corner of the room, I watch one of the richest men on the West Coast waltz across the dance floor with his wife. At least he's not an ass—or hasn't been. Ryan Meltzer introduced himself to each member of the security team when we arrived, apologized for the dress code—tuxedos don't exactly let a guy move freely—and assured us that he'd follow our orders to the letter should anything go wrong.

I resist the urge to snort. The agency—Security Agents For Everyone—or SAFE—vetted tonight's guest list. Meltzer's greatest danger comes from his wife's spiked heels. He's a much better dancer than she is.

Tapping the button hidden inside the jacket sleeve, I relay my own check-in. "Ballroom South—all clear."

Once my counterpart on the north side of the room confirms

he's seen no trouble, I gesture to Meltzer. As the band plays the closing notes of the song, he draws his wife in close, claims her mouth in a lingering kiss, and then laughs when everyone around them bursts into applause and wolf whistles.

"Thank you, ladies and gentlemen. I'm afraid Sarah and I have an early day tomorrow. We're flying to Washington to speak on the behalf of all underprivileged youth in America. Please, enjoy the open bar and don't forget to call your congressperson."

Meltzer waves to the crowd as he and his wife glide off the floor. I resist the urge to check my watch. Six hours on alert, surrounded by tired music, Seattle's business elite clinking glasses of champagne and tossing back shots, and droning speeches leaves me needing two aspirin and a double cheeseburger.

Phillips, a former marine and the owner of SAFE, shakes my hand as Meltzer's car service whisks him out of the country club parking lot. "Thanks for filling in, Sampson. Grab an application when you come pick up your check tomorrow. I'd love to have you on my roster—officially. I can bump you up to thirty bucks an hour once you've passed the background check."

My pride takes a swift kick. A hundred bucks—after taxes—for six hours of work isn't worth the constant pressure of a tie around my neck, the throbbing pain of a cheap earbud in my ear, and the loss of repeated nights talking—or making love to—Cam.

As I pull away from the drive-thru and my stomach rumbles, I swallow the last bit of resolve I had.

"I knew you'd call." The deep voice on the other end of the line carries a hint of bemusement and a truckload of exhaustion.

I take a deep breath to keep from hanging up on the arrogant ass. "You win, Ryker. Set up a meeting with your team."

THOUGHTS OF CAM keep me going until I collapse into bed well after one in the morning. I can't sleep until I call her. Except...she doesn't deserve my shitty mood.

Fuck.

Three text messages wait for me.

Just got home and changed into my robe. And nothing else. Wish you were here.

Now that you're thinking about me naked, I need a favor.

Missed you tonight. Headed to bed, call me first thing tomorrow?

Before I can stop myself, I've dialed her number.

"Hey, handsome," she says, then yawns in the cutest high-pitched moan. "Long night?"

"You have no idea…" My screen flickers to life as Cam connects to FaceTime, and I can't remember what I'd been about to say. Her breasts threaten to spill out of a black tank, her hair curls over her bare shoulders, and in the dim light, her eyes shine.

"West?" She frowns, and I ache to wrap my arms around her, to feel her curves mold against me, to taste her. "Can I see you?"

With a deep breath I hope centers me, I tap the video button. "Better, angel?" I try to smile, but I must not be very successful, because she cocks her head and adjusts her grip on the phone.

"You're tired. I thought you were just working a country club party. Did something happen?"

The concern in her voice smooths the rough edges of my mood. "No. Nothing. The band couldn't even play any good music. I don't know why the guy hired us. The only danger in that room came from the salmon mousse. By the end of the night, it smelled rank."

She laughs, deep and raspy, and her eyes unfocus for a moment before she stretches and shows off a bit of her toned stomach. "Can I see more of you?" she asks and then slides one strap of her tank off her shoulder.

The sheet tents as I imagine her in my bed. Ripping off her tank. Sliding her panties down her long legs. I angle the phone so she can see my abs, and then—as much as I hate myself a little for it—do a half-crunch to define the muscles. Her appreciative purr encourages me to slide my free hand lower, and I show her as my fingers dip under the sheet and wrap around my shaft.

"God, Cam. You have no idea how much I wish you were here."

"If I were there, my mouth would be where your hand is right now. I'd start by caressing the tip with my tongue, slowly. Once. Twice."

I groan. Her hair would cover her face, but I'd smell her— cinnamon and gardenia and aroused woman.

"Then I'd take you in my mouth, using my tongue to trace the underside of your cock. With one hand, I'd guide you deeper, and with the other, I'd cup your balls." She writhes on the bed, grinding her hips against the mattress. She's miles away and I can smell her like she's right next to me.

"How does that feel?"

My dick throbs in my hand, and the tip is already leaking as my fingers do a poor job of replacing her mouth. "Don't stop, angel."

Her eyes glitter as she watches me. "Then, I'd start to suck. Hollow out my cheeks, let you think I'm about to pull off, but then I'd go down again, harder, faster. I'd hum when you were at your deepest, then, for good measure, I'd probably trail my fingernails along your inner thighs."

I feel everything. Every sensation, even the soft locks of her hair brushing my hips. When she moans, the vibration rockets directly to my shaft, and my balls tighten.

"Come for me, West. Come so I can taste you."

With a strangled cry that might have been her name, I follow orders. Cum spurts up my stomach to my chest, and I can't help the jerk of my hips.

"See, if I were there, I'd take care of that for you." Her voice drops another few notes. "Then…" The phone angle changes, and her hand dips into her panties.

I almost lose my grip on the phone as she gasps and her hips start to roll. "Easy, angel. Slow down. I want this to last. Let me see your fingers." She obeys, and even on the small screen, they glisten. "What do you want, Cam?"

"Fuck me, West. Take me and make me scream."

"Oh, you'll be screaming soon enough. Touch yourself. Slowly. Slide your fingers along the edges of where my lips should be right now." As she delves back under the red lace, she moans and my cock starts to throb again. "Good girl. If I were there, I'd slide lower, exploring. Maybe I'd dip one finger inside you. You're so wet, sweetheart."

She gasps again as she follows my running commentary, and her stomach quivers.

"Find the spot, angel. I'm tasting you now, my tongue tracing that hard nub. You're sweet, like honey and rain. God, you're so fucking hot. Faster now. I can't get enough of you."

I'm ready again, and as I palm my shaft, I can barely maintain my grip on the phone. "I'm inside you now. Two fingers curling deep, taking you higher."

We're both panting, and as Cam whimpers my name, I rush to the edge of the precipice. Her phone slips from her grip, and I only catch her hips bucking against her hand. Her cry, half-scream, half strangled groan sends me falling with her.

"West."

I don't know how long I've been staring at the ceiling, but her quiet voice brings me back, and I snag my t-shirt off the floor to clean myself up. "God, Cam. I can't wait for tomorrow." Picking up the phone so I can see her again, I sober immediately. "What's wrong?"

She bites her bottom lip for a moment, squeezes her eyes shut, and runs a hand through her tangled tresses. "Work isn't going well. Royce...something's going on with him."

"Your boss?"

"My former CO, too. We used to be close. Now...he won't talk to me." Her voice cracks, and does her chin wobble? Damn video. I can't tell. "He's been off for weeks, and everyone's noticed. He's called a happy hour for tomorrow—after work. I can't bail. Not—"

"You need to reschedule our date."

"Please don't hate me."

Her unsteady voice suggests she thinks I might. "Angel, we just had mind-blowing sex over FaceTime. You could call me an ugly son of a bitch with garlic breath and tell me you think my sheets came from the dollar bin at the clown store and I wouldn't hate you. But if I don't get you tomorrow night, I have one request."

Her gaze pierces mine through the camera. "Anything."

"Well, I *was* going to say I wanted you all day and all night on Saturday, but now that you've dangled the possibility of anything…"

Her cheeks flush, and a nervous laugh bubbles up. "Shit. I'm going to regret this, aren't I?"

My first genuine smile of the night eases the strain of the past few hours. "I promise to go easy on you. So what do you say? All day and night?"

"I'm yours." She quirks a brow. "What are we doing?"

"A man's got to have some secrets. I'll pick you up at eleven—with coffee. After that, it's need to know."

"Bastard." She grins and pulls the covers up to her chin. "Just for that, no more peep show for you." An odd expression flickers over her features, but before I can ask her if she's all right, she settles back against the pillows with a sigh. "I couldn't sleep before you called—and now I'm too aroused. Tomorrow's going to be one long-ass day."

"Why couldn't you sleep?"

"This job is getting to me. I don't understand. My code was running flawlessly until this week. Now, all of a sudden, whenever I try to test it on the new server we bought for the hotel, it wigs out on me. With Lucas supervising the cabling, I don't have anyone to help me figure this out, and I'm stumped."

"I don't know crap about programming. I can handle a

universal remote and my Xbox, but that's about it. But when I'm frustrated and I can't see my way clear, sometimes taking a step back helps. I'm wiped, but we could play a little *Call of Duty* if you think it'd help."

"I wish. Save that for the weekend. I'll own that tight ass of yours."

"I'm counting on it."

CAM

Nursing my second glass of scotch, I watch Lucas flirt with the bartender. His shoulders shake with laughter, and he tucks a dread behind his ear as the tattooed man with a beard to rival the hippest of hipsters mixes Lucas's manhattan. With happy hour long over, and the rest of the company gone, I asked Lucas to have another round with me. By the time his drink sloshes into the glass, he's jotting digits on a cocktail napkin. He floats back to the table, a silly grin plumping his cheeks.

"Smooth, Luc. You think he'll call?"

His phone buzzes on the table, and Lucas glances at the device, then back at the bartender. "Just did." He types a quick reply and then tucks his phone away. "You sure you don't need to go see lover boy?"

"You just want me to cut you loose so you can go back to flirting." I brush my finger over the rim of my glass, the tumbler warming in my hand. "We need to talk about the other day."

The easy camaraderie we'd enjoyed with the rest of the company around us slips away, and Lucas purses his lips as he stares over my shoulder. My discomfort festers as I wait, and desperate for a distraction, I glance around the crowded bar. The awkward first date behind us can't get past a discussion of the guy's new computer, while to our left, three women toast with the brightest blue drinks I've ever seen and complain about the lack of eligible bachelors their age. When Lucas meets my gaze again, sadness lingers. "You're going to tell Royce, aren't you?"

"No. But if you're really planning on leaving, you have to tell him soon." I settle back in my chair, trying for my best boss stare. "You heard him tonight. Emerald City only works if we're all invested. As soon as this job's done, we need to finalize the facial recognition module for ZoomWare. With the state Oversight's in right now, I won't be able to do that unless I have a kick-ass programmer at my side." I soften my tone as his eyes have taken on a bit of a shimmer. "I want you to run the install."

He fiddles with the cherry stem jutting from his drink, and I have to strain to hear his next words. "You wanted me to handle all the debugging for Coana. Look how that turned out."

"I know. I'm sorry. Royce made the call, but..." Shame flushes my cheeks, mixing with the warmth from the scotch. "I'll talk to him—get him to promise he'll never ask you to pull cable again."

"That's not enough." At my frown, he sighs heavily. "I suck. I know. Royce gave me a job when no one else would. I owe him for that. You too, as I'm pretty sure you went to bat for me."

"I just told him what a fan-fucking-tastic coder you were. Nothing more." The situation's slipping through my fingers, and I can't manage to say the one thing I want to. *I'm sorry I let you down.*

He takes a sip of his drink, nods, and turns his attention to the napkin under his glass. "You've taught me a lot, Cam. Got me on VetNet, helped me work through some of my demons. And you gave me a chance to get certified in Python, turned my rusty skills into something marketable, helped me write my first app. I love working with you. But I'm always going to be second fiddle."

"No, you're not. Luc, we're about to have more clients than we know what to do with. Once word of Oversight gets out and we have a couple of glowing testimonials, I'll need you to take the lead on multiple projects—and I won't be there to back you up because I'll be dealing with projects of my own."

"Even so...Oversight is your system. Your code. Sure, Emerald City owns it, but if things go the way we all hope, the world is going to know that Camilla Delgado is the genius behind it." The passion in his voice surprises me, but he's right, and I don't have an easy retort. "I want my own Oversight. Something that's just mine."

I nod, twisting my napkin in my lap. "When did you start looking for another job?" I don't want to know, don't want to face the fact that Lucas didn't feel he could talk to me. I can count my friends on one hand, and right now, I feel like I'm losing him.

"Two months ago." He looks away, and a muscle ticks in his jaw. "After the Food King job."

I cringe, then finish the rest of my scotch in a single swallow, the alcohol burning as much as Lucas's secrets. "You saved my ass on that one."

Lucas traces a furrow in the scarred wood of the table. "I wanted to prove myself. I thought if I did everything right, Royce would give me my own project. Catching that unhandled exception was pure luck."

"Without the Coana job, he would have." Even I hate how empty my words sound.

He shrugs and his broad shoulders hunch slightly. "With my history…can you blame him for passing me over?"

"Yes. That was years ago."

"I put a man in the hospital, Cam. I went to jail. How do you think that looks to a potential employer? Royce only hired me because you vouched for me. Don't bother denying it."

"You served your time. That has to be worth something." I'm reaching, I know. But Lucas doesn't deserve to continue to pay for a single mistake. Neither do I, but I long ago gave up hope of reconciling with my family.

Lucas shakes his head. "Maybe not, but employers are always going to see my past before my skills. I'm ready for a fresh start. Even so, I don't know that anyone's going to make me an offer once they do a background check. I never expected TechLock to call. Or Software Associates. Or Jilba."

"You deserve every one of those interviews. We've all done

things we're not proud of. Hell, I can't even talk to my father anymore. My mother only contacts me on my birthday, and she always tells me how much of a disappointment I am."

With a snort, Lucas reaches over and pats my hand. "Honey, I've done more to disappoint my mama than almost anyone in this bar." He chuckles. "You should have seen her face when I came out. I was shaking like a leaf in a hurricane."

"You never told me that story." His easy admission soothes my raw nerves, and I try for a smile.

"She came home from church and caught me buck-ass naked with Paulie Tyrell sucking my dick. Kind of hard to pretend to be straight after that." Lucas grins, and a faraway look settles in his eyes. "Mama tanned my hide. Not for being gay, but for skipping church and lying to her. Didn't speak to me for a week. Longest seven days of my life. I never kept a damn thing from her again."

Memories of my own personal hell float to the surface. My father's cold fury, my mother's tears. *Not now.* "I wish I'd known her."

"She was the sweetest woman you'd ever meet—unless someone tried to hassle me. Then, she'd rival the toughest soldier on the battlefield." Lucas catches the eye of the bartender again, winks, and then reluctantly returns his gaze to me.

Catching the hint, I push away from the table and sling my bag across my chest. "I've got to get home. If I want to have any sort of a weekend, I've got to find out why Oversight keeps crashing."

He reaches for my arm. "Let me help."

When I hesitate, his voice turns pleading. "Honey, I'm dying spending my days crawling through ducts filled with cobwebs and layers of dust so thick, the dust bunnies have mutated into horses. I need to get my hands back into the code."

Tears burn the corners of my eyes, and I blink hard to keep them from spilling over. I hate that exhaustion has turned me into an emotional wreck, but between late nights talking—or having insanely hot FaceTime sex—with West and Oversight's rapidly multiplying bugs, I'm stretched so thin I fear I'll snap in two.

"I'll send you the card reader module. Find out what's eating up all the system resources, okay?"

Relief softens his shoulders, and he stands and wraps his arms around me. I sink against his bulk, so happy to have my friend back, I don't even care how hard I have to work to replace his programming skills or how strange the office is going to feel without him.

"Now let me go," I say as I give his shoulder a light shove. "That bartender of yours looks like he's about to go off shift. Maybe you should offer to buy him a drink. Don't even think of starting the debugging until tomorrow."

Lucas turns his gaze to the bar. "Oh, honey. That fabulous man needs much more than a single drink."

DRUNK CODING ISN'T SMART, but at least by the end of the night, I've managed to track down one of the bugs causing Oversight to go belly up at regular intervals. "There you go, baby," I croon as I check in the latest code changes. "Be nice to mama, will you?"

If only she'd listen to me. Another fault flickers across the screen, and I curse. The clock ticks past midnight as I make myself a cup of coffee and then cast a longing stare towards my bedroom. I don't flop into my recliner—I fall—and once I've rubbed my gritty eyes, I launch the debugger again.

The buzzing phone doesn't register until the device dances off the table and hits the floor with a thud. "Dammit."

I'm getting worried. Let me know you're okay.

Three other unread messages wait for me. Shit.

Can't wait until tomorrow, angel. Missed you tonight. I tried Call of Duty *and got my ass kicked.*

Sorry for the late change in plans, but can you meet me at my dojo at ten? I can't get away earlier, and I'd like to show you something.

You still alive?

Once the call connects, I launch into a heartfelt apology.

Though I'm so tired, I'm not sure I'm capable of conveying any emotion. "I've been debugging for the past four hours. Didn't even hear my phone vibrate until just now. I'm so sorry, West."

The strain in his tone belies his next words, "My job last night, yours tonight. Don't worry, angel. It's my turn to ask for a favor, though. Do you mind meeting me at the dojo?"

"Of course not. I'd love to see it." Oversight beeps as she crashes again, and I try, unsuccessfully, to muffle my curse. "If this code doesn't murder me overnight."

"I'm sure you'll beat it into submission. I'll see you in the morning."

No questions, no elaborating? Something's definitely wrong.

"West? Are you okay?" I set my laptop aside and close my eyes, trying to imagine him in bed, wishing I had the time and the energy for a repeat of our previous FaceTime session. "I didn't mean to ignore you—"

"It's not that, Cam. I promise. Just a bad night. Don't stay up too late. You're going to need your stamina this weekend."

I hang up after promising to get some rest, worry over his lack of enthusiasm driving me deep into Oversight's code again. Despite her problems, at least here, I understand the rules.

10

CAM

*L*arge windows look out over the street, and inside, half a dozen men and women wipe down mats while others heft duffel bags or drape towels over their shoulders as they head for the door.

West's dojo holds a corner spot in South Lake Union, but as I lock my car, a huge "Grand Opening" sign across the street catches my eye. Cross Your Fit, with its industrial design and big, bright lights showcasing hard bodies and gleaming equipment, is full, a thumping bass beat so loud, I can feel the vibration in my chest from a hundred feet away.

West's unassuming shop, the punching bags hanging on one side, mats covering the other, doesn't hold the same excitement., though, before my injuries, I'd have loved a place like this.

The pretty young woman at the front desk greets me with a smile. "How can I help you?" When she glances down at my cane, she adds, "Are you here to sign up for the Horizon program? The upcoming session is only for kids, but if you'd like to put your name on the waiting list, I can notify you when our adult accessible classes are open for sign-ups."

She's so earnest that I can't muster any anger. Besides, it's not like I can manage to punch, kick, and grapple anymore. West never mentioned anything about accessible classes, though. Is this why he asked me down here rather than picking me up at home?

"No. I'm a friend of West's."

"Ah." A knowing smile reveals her dimple. "Down the hall, first door on the left." She turns her attention to one of the sweaty customers as I skirt the soft mats. Too many late nights and not enough time in the pool has left me stiffer than usual, and I meet several stares with my best "what the hell are you looking at?" glare. West's office door is cracked, and his voice carries into the hall.

"Look, I've got fifteen kids signed up already, and I'm about to announce the adult program. I can't cancel Horizon now. You promised me if I paid by the end of the month, you'd discount the premiums." He falls silent, and I peer through the narrow opening. Leaning against his desk, his back to me, his head sags forward as he blows out a breath. "Fine." He jabs the screen, then mutters, "Fucking bastards."

As he tosses the phone next to his keyboard, I clear my throat. "West?"

The tension melts from his body as he turns, and when he smiles, I adjust my grip on my cane, as I've suddenly gone a little weak in the knees. In three strides he's in front of me, and then I'm in his arms, unable to stop myself from moaning as he claims my lips and slides a hand up my back.

With how we left things the previous night, I half-expected him to pull away, but the heat in his kiss reassures me that we're solid.

"I should take you right here on the desk," he murmurs in my ear when he comes up for air.

"Does that door lock?" Though I'd pay dearly for the acrobatics necessary to fuck him on a piece of office furniture, I'm not sure I can wait for tonight.

He cups my cheek, his palm warm and smooth against my skin. "Yes, but there's no soundproofing, and you're not exactly quiet when you come."

Flames race up my cheeks, and I step back, unable to hold his gaze any longer. Desperate to redirect the conversation, I grasp for a safe topic. "The woman at the front desk asked me if I was here to sign up for your new 'accessible' classes. What did she mean?"

He blushes and shoves his hands into his pockets. "After I joined VetNet, I got a message from an amputee—WonderLT?—who asked me if I knew of any gyms like mine that took on clients with missing limbs. So I started poking around. I found a few that have personal trainers with experience, but none that offer classes. And nothing at all for kids."

"And you decided to change that?" This man is too good to be real. My heart stutters as he nods.

"We're supposed to launch the new program next month. A six-week 'camp' for kids, and if that goes well, a second kids' camp and a twice-a-week class for adults. My instructors and I have all worked with physical therapists to help us adapt our workouts for amputees, the blind, and people with balance problems." He frowns and glances back at the phone on the desk. "The insurance premiums are going to eat me alive, though. Once you get kids involved, the prices skyrocket. Kids with special needs—an extra five grand a month."

Supposed to launch. Not going to launch. His words play on repeat as I run my hands up his arms. "That's why the CrossFit place—"

"Yeah. I was counting on those membership fees to pay the bills. I've thrown everything I have into this place." West pulls me close, and for a moment, I think I'm all that's holding him upright. He breathes deeply, his nose buried in my soft curls, and when he draws back to meet my gaze, he's smiling once more. "Hey, want to test out a few moves for me?"

"Wh-what?" His one-eighty leaves me reeling, as does the suggestion that I'm in any shape to test out a few moves. "I can't." Tightening my fingers on my cane, I swallow hard, hating that I have to wipe that grin off his handsome face. "What you do here... I wish I could join in. I don't just have balance problems, though. My left leg is too weak to support me on my bad days—and today is a bad day. Unless you've got a couple of 'moves' that can be done seated—"

"More than a couple. A whole class of them." He quirks a brow in invitation, and damnit if I don't want to feel...useful.

Before I realize what I'm doing, my hand finds his, and I let him guide me out the door and into the hall.

"I trained with a few members of the Israeli military between tours," he says as we enter the main room. "Fell in love with Krav Maga—the sheer power and efficiency. Anyone can learn to protect themselves."

I pause, unprepared for the silence of the studio. In the few minutes we spent in his office, everyone cleared out. Even the blonde at the front desk. The scent of cleanser hangs in the air, and the thick windows insulate us from the thumping bass across the street.

"You closed for the day?"

"Until 5:00 p.m. The afternoon classes don't draw enough of a crowd to pay an instructor." His voice roughens, and when he meets my gaze, strain tightens his eyes. Sparing one long look at the CrossFit studio, he shakes his head. "Fuckers."

Once he's kicked off his shoes, West grabs a chair from the side of the room and then sets it in the center of the thick, blue mats. He eases my cane from my hand. "I won't let you fall."

I can't help the momentary panic as he leads me across the squishy floor. I hate mats. But curiosity wins out over nervousness, and once I'm seated, the floor-to-ceiling mirrors reveal a hint of excitement on both of our faces.

West brushes his lips against my cheek, sending goosebumps peppering my bare arms. "Krav Maga teaches you how to use your own strength as an advantage. No matter how much stronger your opponent is." He steps in front of me and rests his hands along my collar bone. "If I tried to strangle you, what would you do?"

Slowly, he slides his hands closer, never tightening his grip or breaking eye contact, but still, my heart stutters, and I fight to keep my breathing calm. I grab his wrists, trying to pull his hands down, and then to the sides, but he's too strong. "West."

As he lets go, I draw an unsteady breath, and he drops to his knees, wraps his arms around me, and lets me lean against him. "I'm sorry. I should have let you do that to me first."

"I'm okay…" I want to be, but though I haven't trusted anyone in a long time like I trust him, my heart still pounds.

"Look at me, Cam." When I meet his gaze, concern darkens his eyes. "Nothing's going to happen to you when I'm around. I promise. If you don't want to continue, we can go kayaking."

He looks so sincere, I can't wimp out, nor do I want to. "I get to strangle you?"

With a laugh, he nods. "Try. Both hands."

I'm not sure what he's hoping to prove, but at least this doesn't require me to fight against some irrational self-preservation instinct, so I wrap both hands around his neck. "What now?"

"Don't let me pull your hands away."

"Yeah, right." I lock out my muscles, and to my surprise, he struggles to remove my hands. When he releases my wrists, he sits back on his heels.

"You've got great shoulders and lats, Cam. Swimming gives you more upper body strength than most women. Even without that, pulling someone's hands down or to the side is the least efficient method of breaking a choke hold. Try again, and this time, use as much strength as you can. You won't hurt me."

When he straightens, I return my hands to his throat. How he's not panicking, I don't understand, as I can feel him swallow against my grip, but he smiles, the light in his eyes reassuring me. In a single breath, my hands fly apart, and I don't even know how he broke free. "What did you do?"

He nods and I try again. This time, he slows his movements. As he jams his hands upwards against my wrists, my hold breaks. "There are two weak points in any choke hold: the wrists and the shoulders. Force one of those to bend, and you can easily get free. Most people try to pull down. That's working against your opponent's strength: their lats and abs."

"Can I try?" Though I trust him, my breath quickens when he wraps his hands around my neck. Despite the tension in his biceps, when I snap my arms up and hit his wrists, his hands shoot up and away. "Shit."

"That's the first move we teach in self-defense. Even if you only have one arm, you can usually escape a choke hold with that technique. Want to try something else?"

He's excited now, but so am I. "Yes."

When I master a second technique—defending against a frontal attack—West ends up flat on the ground, the assailant turned victim, and the rush of adrenaline fills me with longing. I ease myself down, the thick mats allowing me to straddle him, my hands braced on his sculpted chest, the heat of him no match for my desire set aflame.

"Watch out, angel. Don't tempt me if you're not *very* sure about this." He licks his lips, and the few reservations I have fly out the window. Since we're hidden from view by the heavy bags, I strip off my tank.

"Your move."

He pulls me down, his erection pressing into my hip. "Last chance."

"Fuck me, West. Please." He's gentle as he eases my shorts down my hips, then with a final glance towards the mostly-hidden door, he straightens. His abs ripple as he strips off his shirt, and when he's naked, I wrap my fingers around his cock, stroking the length as he shudders in my grip.

I intend to continue my ministrations, but he reaches down and pinches my nipple through my black lace bra, and the shock of pain sends a rush of need shooting through my core. My back arches as I release him, and he slides a finger under the hem of my panties, teasing my center.

Moaning as I thrust my hips closer to his hand, I'm rewarded by exquisite pressure against my mound. Too soon, he pulls away but then yanks my panties down my legs. "I want to taste you."

I'd give anything in the world to feel his tongue against my clit, but he offers freely, and as his hands frame my hips and he starts to lap at my folds, stars twinkle at the edge of my vision. I can't breathe, can't hold on, and when he scrapes his teeth along the throbbing bundle of nerves, white hot pleasure implodes within me. I can't hear myself scream, can't see or sense anything besides West. He tugs on a condom and as he pulls my hips up, sliding his cock deep inside in a single, swift move, I claim his lips.

With my arousal sweet on his tongue, I can't get enough of him, and I rock my hips closer, though he threatens to split me in two. So lost in the pleasure building again, I don't even notice when he breaks the kiss, but as his teeth close over my nipple, I arch, and the movement urges his cock just where I need him to be. Keening cries reach my ears, and I don't recognize them as my own until he kisses me again and the sound fades.

Our sweat-slicked bodies move with a punishing rhythm, each thrust taking me higher. When I don't think I can stand another moment, West reaches down and flicks my clit. I fly apart, and a heartbeat later, he joins me.

WEST

Lights twinkle all along the Seattle Wheel. Why the city decided to erect a Ferris Wheel on the waterfront I'll never understand, but the red, white, and blue lights—leftover from the 4th of July, make for a romantic backdrop as I slide my hand down Cam's back.

After kayaking on Lake Union, I brought her to the Pinball Museum, where I learned to never bet against her. Down eight games to one, I wagered the rest of the night on a single run of an obscure Lord of the Rings machine.

"Truth now, angel. You let me win that last game, didn't you?"

She glances up at me, her dark brown eyes nearly black as the last purple streaks in the sky fade into the night. "I don't know what you're talking about." A hint of a smile curves her lips. "That dwarf came out of nowhere to redirect my ball."

Pausing at the railing so we can stare out over Elliot Bay, I draw her against me—her back pressed to my chest, my arms around her waist. "When I'm with you, nothing else matters."

She turns and tips her face up. Our lips are only inches apart, and the hint of aroused woman tickles my nose. Her brows draw together in confusion, and I ache to smooth the wrinkle away. "West, last night, you were—"

Her mouth curves into a frown, and I slide my fingers into her hair, pull her closer, and crush my lips to hers. If I go back to last night, I'll stay there, in the dark and despair of one too many nightmares, one too many bills to pay. My time with Cam is too precious. She tastes of the scotch we ordered with dessert, along with a hint of chocolate. As I deepen the kiss, she yields to my desires—and her own. Short nails scrape over my shoulders, down my back, and when she grinds her hips against me, I can't help my groan.

"You won the bet. What do you want to do now?" She palms the painful bulge in my cargo shorts, glancing around quickly to ensure no one's watching our rather public foreplay.

"God, Cam." I can't think when she touches me. "Let's get out of here. ..."

STRETCHED OUT ON HER SIDE, her arms wrapped around one of my pillows, Cam sighs in her sleep. The blindfold and soft cuffs I bought on a hunch hang from the headboard, the memory of her screaming my name, her hands gently bound above her head soothing the monster inside me. How can I sleep knowing I could wake up to find myself on the floor, huddled in my closet, or worse—with a weapon in my hands ready to fight?

I brush a kiss to her bare shoulder. "I'm falling for you, angel. Might be halfway to loving you."

She stirs at my whisper, but settles again without opening her eyes. With the hours she's been working lately, she needs the sleep, so I grab my pillow and settle on the floor next to the bed. I've half a mind to sleep on the couch, but the less comfortable I am, the less likely I am to have nightmares. Survivor's guilt, my therapist says.

One quick stretch to flick off the lamp, and darkness blankets the room, broken only by the single shaft of moonlight illuminating my angel.

WAVES OF PAIN race up my legs, my ankle shattering as I fall through the floor to the hard-packed dirt below. I grunt, ignoring the agony. If you can't hoof it a mile on a broken leg, you're not cut out to be a SEAL. At least that's what my CO always said. Something rattles next to me, and I'm instantly on alert, coming to a crouch, only then realizing I'm naked. In my bedroom. Prepared to defend myself against the nightstand.

"West?" Cam's sleepy voice penetrates the thick smoke that threatens to choke me. "Where are—?"

Shaking my head, I clear the last vestiges of the nightmare. Smitty isn't really dead two feet away, the room isn't burning around me, and the primary scent in the room isn't blood, but Cam. My ass hits the floor, and when my head slams into the nightstand, the lamp rattles.

"Down here."

Sheets rustle, followed by a muffled curse, and then she's looking down at me, her mussed curls tangled around her face. "Are you sleeping on the floor?"

Thick strands of carpet dig into my knees as I stretch to flip on the light. "Yeah." The lump in my throat strangles my reply, and I clear my throat. "Just...easier."

"Easier?" Her voice lowers, her slight accent thickens. With a groan, she eases herself off the bed and starts limping around for her clothes. "We don't have to sleep together. I can go home."

"No." My plea sounds rougher than I intend, and she stops with her panties clutched in her hand. "I get nightmares, Cam. All the time. Hell, I haven't had a woman in my bed overnight for two years. I didn't want to hurt you." I can't look at her, but warm fingers wrap around my wrist and tug me up to the mattress.

"Look at me," she says. "I didn't get a solid night's sleep for three years after the bombs. Between the pain and the nightmares, I resembled a zombie—all the shuffling, groaning, and inability to form coherent sentences. A few more months, and I probably would have developed a taste for brains."

After a pause, she jabs me in the arm with her elbow. "Oh, come on. That was a little funny." When I meet her worried gaze with a weak grin, she reaches over to cup my cheek. "I know nightmares. The meds help with the arthritis and the nerve pain, but nothing erases the terror of being unable to move while fire eats through your protective gear. Nightmares don't frighten me."

She'd never explained how she'd been hurt—just "blown up trying to diffuse a bomb." The ghosts of fear play in her eyes, and I wrap my arms around her naked body, relishing in the feel of her soft, warm curves against my chilled skin.

"I could hurt you. I've woken at the foot of the bed, even across the room. When I have a serious attack, I find the sheets and pillows on the floor. What if I kick you?" Barely able to manage a whisper, I grit my teeth to stop myself from shivering.

"Then you'll have to drive me home and carry me into my condo, where you'll wait on me hand and foot for the few hours it takes my meds to kick in."

She's grinning now, but I can't help flinching, and her smile fades. "West, there are a lot of things I can't do." She ticks them off on her fingers. "Dancing, running, mountain climbing, snowboarding… But I'm not fragile. I have pain. With all of the titanium, staples, and plastic in my body, I'm almost indestructible. Trust me."

I *know* she's not a china doll. Not a broken bird who needs protecting. Doesn't stop me from wanting to try. I nod, then snag my pillow off the floor. Once I've turned off the light, I stretch out on my back, as far from Cam as the king bed will allow.

"Not much better." Her hand slides over my abs, and her arm brushes my shaft.

"Cam, I don't think—"

"Maybe you need some incentive." She hums, halfway between a sigh and a moan as she drapes her luscious body on top of mine. At the first swivel of her hips, I'm lost.

"Don't start something…you can't finish." Aching to bury myself deep inside her, I cup her breast, drag my thumb over her peaked nipple.

She feathers kisses along my neck, closes her teeth over my ear lobe, and grinds her hips again. "Oh," she whispers against my cheek, "I can finish. Indestructible, remember?"

CAM

*W*est's bedroom looks out over a verdant backyard, and we're on our second cup of coffee in bed when I trail my fingers over the stars and stripes that arc across his ribs. Names unfurl in an almost delicate script: Fox, Baxter, Hawk, and Smitty.

"Your team?"

He sucks in a breath, making the flag twitch under my hand. For a long moment the only sound in the room is his ragged breathing as his skin chills under my touch. "The ones I—we—lost. The entire squad." After a sip of coffee, he sets the mug aside with a vaguely ill grunt and draws his leg up to rest an elbow on his knee. "My last op… Most of what we do—did—is classified. I can't tell you where we were, what our objective was. Not in any detail." He looks to me, seeking approval, and when I nod, he continues. "We were on a rescue mission. Two hostages and four hostiles. Or so we thought. We'd gotten bad intel. Walked into a fucking ambush. We'd trained for this, so we cleared the rooms one by one, taking heavy fire. Until the last room. They'd secured the hostages in a bedroom, down a long hall. The hostiles set off a bomb that brought down the building. Knocked me out, and when I came to, I couldn't feel my arm." He reaches for my hand, guiding my fingers to a thick scar just above his armpit. "Piece of rebar shattered the collar bone, pinned me to the floor. The hostages were dead, along with three of my men and a seventy-five-year-old woman and her granddaughter who were there as decoys. The last member of my team, Smitty, bled out in front of me."

Silence stretches between us, and he's shaking, trapped in the memory. He doesn't see me; his eyes are unfocused, watching his friend—his fellow SEAL—die all over again. I wrap my arms around him, but still, he trembles, and a keening moan escapes his pale lips. "West. Come back to me. Please." I kiss him, run my hands up and down his arms. When he struggles free and meets my gaze, I tangle our legs under the blanket. "Were you in charge?"

With a heavy sigh, he nods. "Led dozens of missions before that last one, and while we had some failures, no one had died under my watch until that day. The navy asked me if I'd come back, but I couldn't. Not after failing my squad. Four funerals, four grieving families—not to mention the dead hostages. Put in for my discharge before I'd even left the hospital."

The skin of his back is cool under my palm, and I try to weigh what I'm supposed to say against what I'd feel if I were in his place. "Did you break protocol? Ignore a direct order or clear intel?"

"No." He meets my gaze, and the raw anguish that churns in the depths of his eyes twists my gut. "In my head, I know I'm not to blame. I've replayed that day a thousand times—and I live through it again most nights. The insurgents fed us lies, and someone higher up believed them. I still see Smitty lying in a pool of his own blood, gasping for breath, begging me to tell his mother that he loved her. No amount of therapy can erase that horror. You understand, don't you?"

Three times I open my mouth to tell him what happened to me, but I can't. The pain wells up, and the lump in my throat threatens to choke me. Burnt flesh, smoke, the bitter scent of blood mixed with sand and dust surround me, tinging the beautiful spring day a dark copper—the color of the innards of my ruined bomb suit melting into my skin. He waits for my answer, and as the seconds tick by, my silence adds more bricks to the wall I've so carefully erected over the years.

When I shock myself out of my hesitation, I nod—too quickly —and fiddle with the hem of the t-shirt he lent me. "After the bombs went off… They say your life flashes before you. Mine didn't. Not until later. I see myself cutting wires, sweat pouring down my temples, and I wonder if I'd just stepped left instead of right… I can only imagine what my CO felt. Hell, he wouldn't even come to see me in the hospital." Even now, thinking back to the weeks I spent in that uncomfortable bed, each member of my team rotating in to visit to try to keep my spirits up, Royce's absence crushes me.

"Tell me what happened?" He strokes his hand down my bare thigh, over part of my leg I haven't felt in ten years. I can't do this. Not now. Instead of talking, I lean in and crush my lips to his, offering him everything I am—or at least everything I'm able to give.

Cam,

This module's running perfectly for me. No unusual memory spikes or errors. Are you sure the problem isn't somewhere else? I'm going to put in a few hours cabling with the crew, but I can help you out again after 7:00 p.m.

-Lucas

"Shit." I down the remainder of my coffee—grocery store brew that doesn't hold a candle to the macchiatos West made me this morning while naked—and shudder as I tip over the edge from productive to jittery. Four hours of debugging and I'm no closer to fixing Oversight.

Take a look at the HVAC module next. I'm diving back into the core framework. Thanks, Lucas. How are Al and the guys doing?

My laptop beeps as another error pops up on screen, politely informing me that the surveillance cameras will shut down in thirty seconds to conserve system resources. "Come on, baby. Talk to me. Tell me what's got you so tied up in knots."

Half an hour later, a single line of code catches my eye—one I didn't write. Like a treasure map, that line leads to another, and another, and soon I've found half a dozen modules with errors in them. Small, insignificant errors that add up to something much bigger.

Hey Lucas,

You worked on the clean-up module in the main framework, right? There's something funky going on there. Tag me when you get this.

-Cam

After a quick break to order pizza, I check in on VetNet. The PTSD board is hopping, but few messages wait for me anywhere else. I have two missed messages from HuskyFan, so once I send my latest module to the compiler, I open up a private chat.

FlashPoint: *Hey. How's it going? Are you on baby watch yet? I never asked how far along your wife was.*

The little dots at the bottom of the window spin as I crack my neck.

HuskyFan: *She's got another eight weeks. My mother-in-law hates me for working all these extra hours, but in a little over a week, I'll be done with this side job, and I'll be able to afford our insurance. I took the boy to the Science Museum this morning, and he begged me to call in sick tomorrow. Broke my heart, but at least I got to spend a few hours with him before I headed off to my side job.*

FlashPoint: *That's great, HF! Are things going okay at work? Both jobs?*

Again, the dots dance, but this time he stops typing then starts three times again before his message pops up.

HuskyFan: *Yes.*

I frown at all that time messaging for a single word answer. Then again, it's hard to share with virtual strangers, and sometimes, we need to some encouragement to open up.

Before I can reply, Oversight throws up an error. "You little bitch," I mutter as I switch over to the compiler to try to find the problem. The computer dings at me, but other than a cursory glance at the flashing message window, I don't look up for another fifteen minutes. Once I've eliminated the fault and sent the code through again, I find three messages waiting for me, each more concerned than the last.

FlashPoint: *Sorry. Work is killing me right now. You were nervous about taking that side job. Did it turn out to be a good thing?*

Another few minutes pass while I verify that my code changes didn't cause anything else to break.

HuskyFan: *Not something I can really talk about, but the people I'm working for are assholes, and they don't care that I have to work all night. I still don't want to be here, but I don't have much choice. How was your date?*

My cheeks heat, and as I shift in my recliner, all of the little aches and pains from a night—and morning—filled with ecstasy make themselves known.

FlashPoint: *We're going to Portland in a few weeks for a long weekend.*

HuskyFan: *Sounds fun. I took my wife there before we got married.*

On paper, he's right. Three days with my *boyfriend* in one of my favorite cities should make me happy. So why am I vaguely nauseous? Leaning my head back against the chair, I remember West's hands on me, the soft restraints he brought out the previous night, the overwhelming climax I had while blindfolded and unable to move my arms. Maybe this will be fun. Or at least... maybe I won't screw things up.

HuskyFan: *You still there?*

I'm somewhere. Like back in West's bedroom.

FlashPoint: *No. I just... This is getting serious.*

Another few minutes pass as HuskyFan types, and I alternate between worry I've said too much and relief that I can admit my fears to someone—even if it is an anonymous someone on the internet. Lucas doesn't even know the extent of my issues, though he's tried to find out more than once.

HuskyFan: *You like this guy, right? Isn't serious a good thing?*

The pizza delivery guy shows up, and I'm grateful for the time to think of a reply that doesn't make me sound like a commitment-phobic asshole. Though I'm not sure I succeed.

FlashPoint: *I haven't had a long-term relationship in...well...ever? My record is three weeks. Any longer than that, and the guys want you to meet their parents and share secrets. I don't do well with those parts.*

HuskyFan is either typing a book, or he doesn't know what to say. I'm about to tell him to ignore me when his message pops up on the screen.

HuskyFan: *We all have secrets. Even your dude. You said he gets you. Why not just ask him to be patient with you? Or do something really crazy and let him in. What's the worst that could happen?*

I could. Of course, I could. Just open my mouth and confess my painful history. But after our weekend together, I fear we've passed the point where I can admit I don't have a relationship with my parents because I was an idiot sixteen years ago. I run my fingers over one of the thickest scars above my wrist.

FlashPoint: *You don't understand. My family won't talk to me anymore because I did something supremely stupid. My best friend from the army—my CO for fuck's sake—walked out on me after I got blown up. I work for him now. I have to face him every day, and know that I'll never see the old Royce again. The one who used to challenge me to drinking contests, who talked me through every bomb I diffused, who used to give me his MRE brownies because oddly, they reminded me of my Nana's. If this guy learns all of that, how likely do you think he is to stick around?*

Silent tears race down my cheeks. I loved those fucking brownies. The sobs well up, and I slam the lid of the laptop, ashamed. The unbidden confession rips open a wound I thought had long healed, and I rub at one of the scars along my arm as if I can shove the words back inside and erase the memories of asking for Royce in the hospital time and time again when the doctors debated taking my leg.

I stumble into the kitchen, desperate for something to dull the pain—to quash the taste of cinnamon on my tongue—Nana's secret brownie ingredient—or the scent of roses from my mama's perfume. The fiery cascade of bourbon ensures I won't taste a damn thing for a while, and after the second generous pour disappears, I force myself to stopper the bottle. Getting drunk won't solve anything—I'm well aware of that—but the slight buzz has the desired effect. I can breathe again, and now regret seeps in.

I run a shaking hand through my hair and sniffle loudly. Maybe HuskyFan is right. West could hear about my colorful youth and laugh. Or he could be one more person who leaves.

CAM

$\mathcal{T}$he flower vendor grins as she hands me a single daisy. "They're my favorite, too," she says. "Most folks pass 'em over for the roses or the lilies, but daisies can hold their petals for two whole weeks if you treat 'em right."

I twirl the yellow flower in my fingers, the petals blurring as she tells me exactly how to keep the flower fresh. Just a small amount of water, changed often, and sunlight. I can do that. Once today's over. With how little sleep I managed the previous night, I'll have no end of challenges waiting for me in the basement server room. At least this little beauty will keep me company.

As I enter the hotel, my phone buzzes.

I need to see you tonight. Please tell me you'll be up if I come over around 10?

This week promises to try to break me, and I need every minute I can spare to finish Oversight so the testing can begin. With ten days until LaCosta wants the system fully implemented, I'm scrambling, but seeing West...having his arms around me for even a few minutes would be heaven.

I can't promise to be good company.

The phone rings before I can slip the device back into my pocket. "What's wrong?" When I don't immediately answer, West clears his throat, and some of the hoarseness in his voice quiets. "I probably won't be good company either, but we'd be together."

"This job is killing me." I sink down onto one of the plush benches that line the lobby. "Every day, something else breaks. If I can't stop the bleeding, Oversight...everything Royce has built, everything I've worked for these past three years...we'll lose it all."

"I thought you had help. There are other programmers at your firm, right?"

"This is my baby, West. Royce trusted me, and I promised him we'd be okay." Dropping my head into my free hand, I try to shut down the memory of the last promise I made Royce, but my feeble attempt falls flat, and all I can see is his much-younger face, his flack jacket, the helmet that always seemed a little too small for him. "I have to fix Oversight. I don't have a choice."

"You always have a choice, angel. Your options might suck, but you always have a choice." Sadness laces his tone, and I ache to wrap my arms around him. Words fail me, and he sighs. "I've got a class in five minutes. I'll see you tonight?"

"Sure." Only after he hangs up do I realize I never asked him why he wouldn't be good company. Score another "F" for me on the "Caring Girlfriend" report card.

As I adjust my laptop bag, I catch sight of Al heading for the freight elevators. "Al! Hold up a minute."

He stops, turning slowly as I reach his side. "'Morning. Nice flower."

I can't help my smile as I glance at the daisy. "My father used to bring these to my mother all the time, and the flower cart outside had a huge display this morning."

Al shifts from foot to foot as the elevator numbers slowly count down. "I've got to get up to twelve. Lucas is expecting me."

"I'll ride with you." We don't speak again until the doors seal us in, and I can't help noticing his bloodshot eyes as he darts a quick glance in my direction. "You okay?"

He forces a smile. "Fine. Long couple of days. Half the crew and I worked ten hours yesterday. We're headed to thirteen after lunch."

We're almost a floor ahead, and if the guys can keep up this pace, I might get Lucas back in time to help me customize the last two modules. "You're doing great work. I know you're new to the company, but Royce is pretty cool about time off after big projects. You can bank on at least a couple of paid days off once we go live." I step out into the hall and wait for him to join me. "Hang in there a little longer."

"I'll try." His phone trills as he clips his ID card to his belt. "I've got to take this." The thick carpet muffles his footfalls as he practically races down the hall. "I told you I took care of it," he mutters before he turns the corner.

Al's weekend may have sucked, but Lucas is a ray of sunshine. "You wanted results, we've got 'em, hon. All of the cameras on the lower floors are working, and the last batch of hardware is out for delivery."

I high-five him, and the knot in the pit of my stomach eases. We chat for a few minutes, and then he drops his voice to a whisper. "TechLock is supposed to get back to me today."

Boom. The stress crashes down, and I exhale a deep breath, trying to release some of my worry over losing Lucas with a sigh. When I turn to him, a desperate need for approval greets me.

Offering a supportive smile as I shove my own insecurities aside, I pat his arm. "I know they'll love you. Just...don't forget about us when you're all brilliant-project-manager dude knocking them dead with your talent."

He nods, his eyes shining, and I head for the computer room before my emotions run haywire.

Once I'm at my temporary desk surrounded by racks of tall servers, with my daisy in an old to-go cup next to me, I launch the standard systems checks and let my mind wander. Thanks to West,

I'm addicted to those damn macchiatos now, and Broadcast Coffee is only two blocks away. My wallet might be doomed. I even bought a bag of their fancy beans for home. This can only end badly. *Woman goes bankrupt from gourmet coffee habit.* I can see the headlines now.

The harsh beep startles me from my daydreams—mostly involving West and a naked Halo battle where the winner has a can of whipped cream—and I peer at the fault on the monitor. Error messages stack, one after another after another, and I scramble to try to shut the system down. The door to the server room thunders open, and I yelp in surprise.

"What the fuck is going on?" Royce towers over me, and the look in his eyes could melt glass. Or freeze lava. "I was just in LaCosta's office when the call came in. We're eating up a ton of network resources and slowing down his booking system."

"I know. I don't know why. Oversight's got the smallest footprint of any security system on the market today and half of the ones still in development." I push to my feet, though Royce and I will never be on equal footing again. "I check the logs every day, and our network drain has always been minimal."

My heart rate skyrockets as I launch the sophisticated monitoring tools Royce wrote the year before he hired me. Every single gauge redlines within seconds.

"We're fucked." Veins start to throb at his temples. "We're going to lose all of the other Coana properties *and* ZoomWare. We'll be the laughing stock of the entire industry." His tone takes on an accusatory edge. "Why didn't you ask for help?"

I clench my hands hard enough to send tiny needles of pain zinging my palms. "I ran diagnostics on Friday once I installed the first set of modules. Everything was perfect." Fury chills my tone. "Better than perfect, in fact, because I'm a fucking genius with code, and you know it. I didn't get a single alert all weekend. Whatever caused this happened in the past twenty-four hours. So get off my ass and leave me the hell alone. I'll fix this, but I'm not going to do it with you standing watch over me."

"Shut everything down until you do. Everything. Get Lucas in here to help you. Or hell, tell *me* what to do."

I'm already limping over to the network switch. "This isn't my first day on the job." Once I unplug the three cables that connect Oversight to the hotel's network, I brace my hand on the table so I'm not tempted to punch Royce. Years of pent-up anger threaten to spill over in a single moment, and if I let go, I'll lose so much more than I'm prepared for. "You know I work better alone. Go back to the office and let me do my job. I'll find the problem. Tell LaCosta I'm going through the software line by line, and I'll install additional monitoring to guarantee this won't happen again."

He throws up his hands. "Fine. Have it your way. I want a detailed report by the end of the day. In person. Stop by the office on your way home."

I flinch as the door slams again, and my stomach roils. Alone, frustrated, and a little scared, I load the first module and get to work.

BY MID-AFTERNOON, I'm sick. My hands shake with every keystroke, and my stomach burns from too much coffee and not enough food. Two of the original modules are back in production and performing perfectly. The third, however, threatens my sanity —and more.

Royce keeps calling, but I can't talk to him yet. Not without answers. Code unfolds before me, Oversight's guts laid bare for dissection, and I tease out one particular line of code I've seen a dozen times today, but never before. Unless I blacked out—repeatedly—I never would have shuffled the processing like that, and the only other programmer with access—Lucas—should have known better as well.

"Talk to me, baby." I rub the back of my neck to try to release some of the tension, but granite has nothing on my muscles. Every time I try to strip these lines of code from the system, Oversight grinds to a halt. Unable to see my way clear, I break down and text Lucas.

I need you in the server room.

Five minutes. Ten. Twenty. When the phone finally rings, I can't help snapping. "Where the hell are you?"

"I'm on my way to TechLock. They wanted to meet in person and this traffic is killing me. What's wrong?" He honks his horn and swears under his breath.

"The camera control module's all fucked up and it's taking down the whole damn system. Did you work on it this weekend?"

"Cam, I haven't touched a single line of code other than what *you* sent me since Royce put me on cabling. I wrote that module two months ago. You said my work was flawless—the best I'd ever done, remember?"

"Then what happened? Because I can't load the damn thing without the whole system crashing. You and I are the only ones who have access to the source code, and I know you want off cabling." My voice has risen half a dozen notes, and my tenuous grip on my emotions threatens to snap as I scroll through line after line of complete and utter garbage disguised as Oversight's code.

My stomach flips as his tone turns defensive. "Whoa, honey. I've been working my ass off in cramped, hot crawlspaces since we started this project. The spiders know me on sight now. And I *still* found time to help you this weekend. If that's not dedication, I don't know what is. I would never do anything to jeopardize this install and I sure as shit wouldn't hurt my best friend by ruining her career—which if you're not paying attention, is what you just accused me of." His car door slams. "If all goes well, I'll be back to Coana in ninety minutes. We'll figure this out together. After you apologize to me."

If all goes well... The reminder shatters me, and I choke back a sob. "Oversight is my responsibility. I'll fix it. When you're done there, go back to cabling."

"Camilla Delgado, you damn well better not—"

As I end the call, my world crumbles beneath me, and with no one to pick up the pieces, I don't know how to find solid ground again. I can't breathe and push my chair back so I can drop my head between my knees. Where did I go wrong? Did Lucas lie to me? Jeopardize the biggest project of our careers because Royce put him on cabling?

He'd never do that to me.

My eyes start to mist and burn, and I hate myself for even considering the possibility that my best friend would betray me. If only I could see another option. Once the room stops spinning, I reach for my phone, needing an outside perspective. West's voice-mail greets me, and I have to clear my throat twice before I can say anything after that stupid beep.

"I... Something happened. Shit, that sounds so ominous." I can't help the high-pitched squeak that comes out as I try to laugh and fail. "Call me back as soon as you can, please."

Almost as soon as I hang up, I regret the words, so I send him a text.

I just left you a vague voice mail. Consider it a 911 without any of the injuries or danger of death. Something happened with the project I'm working on, and I can't talk to anyone else.

After that message disappears into the ether, I open the backup copy of the camera control module. The whys aren't important now. Oversight has to be my priority. "Okay, baby. Let's find a way to make you whole again."

EACH MINUTE STRETCHES OUT LONGER than the next. Other than the hum of the servers and the *tat-tat-tat* of my typing, I'm surrounded by silence. West hasn't called, I haven't seen Lucas, and even Royce has been quiet since I told him I found the problem and will have a fix and a report for him before I go home tonight.

The clock taunts me: 5:59 p.m., 6:25 p.m., 7:12 p.m. When Lucas trudges in, the look of pure anguish on his face stays my tongue until he speaks.

"I'd much rather go home and open a bottle of chardonnay," he says with a hitch in his voice. "And before you say anything, I finished the cabling on both thirteen *and* fourteen. I didn't touch the camera control module after you approved it, so what the hell happened?" A lone cobweb hangs from one of his dreads, and a rip in his t-shirt exposes a sliver of shoulder.

I'd give anything to not be here right now. To be back on the battlefield, elbow deep in some car bomb with Royce in my ear. I turn my laptop screen so Lucas can see the problem subroutines. "What is this?"

He narrows his eyes, bending down to scrutinize the offending function calls. "I have no idea. That's not my code."

"Well, I know I didn't write it." Shaking my head only aggravates my headache, and I curse under my breath. "The truly sad part? Some of the functions here are fucking brilliant. Better than I could have done. But then I find shit like this. I had to shut down the whole system to stop the memory leaks."

Lucas unzips his messenger bag. "Let me help. Between the two of us, we can strip out all of the bad code in a few hours. And then we can both have wine."

"There's nothing left for you to do." I shut my laptop with a little more force than necessary, then blink hard to battle my watery eyes as I push myself to my feet. "I fixed the last module ten minutes ago. I'll test everything from home."

"Goddammit, Cam. Why won't you let anyone help you?" Lucas pulls hard on handfuls of his dreadlocks. "Can't you see what you're doing?"

"I'm doing my fucking job. I've *been* doing my fucking job ever since LaCosta moved up the deadline." Shouting does nothing for my nerves, but I can't help myself. "I've given up nights, weekends, time with West, and even swimming, just so I can finish this project on time. And what have you done? Interview with half a dozen companies so you can *leave*."

Lucas's voice drops to a whisper. "I put in fifteen hour days this weekend. Ten hours cabling, five hours a night debugging. All to try to save you from yourself."

Squaring my shoulders as best I can with the exhaustion weighing me down, I can't help my harsh tone. "I don't need saving."

"The hell you don't." With a huff, Lucas grabs his messenger bag. "You're so wrapped up in your own shit that you can't even see that Royce needs you."

"Wh-what? Royce doesn't need shit. He's made that abundantly clear." All I can see is Royce's face as he slaps down the flames searing my skin. The horror in his gaze as he tosses aside the car door that landed on my leg, the plea on his lips I can't hear because the explosions shattered my ear drums. My knees turn to jelly, but for once, my injuries have nothing to do with the sensation.

Lucas snorts. "Royce called me last week. Broke down, begged me to talk to you. But you don't let anyone in, Cam. You know every fucking thing about me—down to how many times I ended up in the prison infirmary. But you? I don't even know your mama's first name, your high school sweetheart…or how you got hurt other than 'diffusing a car bomb.'" He shakes his head, lets out a heavy sigh, and wrenches the door open.

"By the way…TechLock ran a background check. The reason they wanted to meet today? The recruiter thought there'd been some mistake. When I told her I'd served my time, she tore the offer up right in front of me. Thanks for asking."

My world shatters as the door slams shut, but I can't muster a single tear. Instead, I sink down to the carpet and start to shake. Lucas was the one person I knew would never leave me. Except… now he's gone, and there's a gaping maw where my heart should be.

I don't know that I can survive this again.

WEST

A rare summer rain shower slicks the empty streets, the lights reflecting off of pools of greasy water alongside a road that's seen better days. This section of south Seattle doesn't stir after 9:00 p.m., unless you count the drug dealers and the occasional prostitute.

Ryker's warehouse looms ahead of me, a dim glow from the large windows on the third story the only sign of life. Below, the building's nothing but cement and steel, a fortress—unbreachable if I know him at all.

Cam's message weighs on me as I shut my phone off. I should have replied, but hearing her voice right now might send me running in the opposite direction of the one hope I have to save the Horizon program and keep my business afloat. Shoving the phone into my glove box, I roll my eyes at the precautions he demanded. No electronics. Nothing traceable. Hell, he wouldn't even tell me the address of this place until he verified my texting app was encrypted.

A whiff of Cam's delicious scent—coffee and lilies— surrounds me as I lock my car. She borrowed one of my t-shirts on Sunday morning, and I'm wearing the damn thing today. Why'd I have to fall so hard and fast? I'm not even sure she wants me—wants a relationship long term—but damn if she isn't it for me.

The steel warehouse door opens a crack as I raise my fist to knock. "Clean?"

"No one followed me." My foul mood doesn't leave much room for stupid questions. "Also, in case you've forgotten, we're in Seattle. Nothing happens here."

Ryker jerks the door wider, grabs my arm, and yanks me inside.

Anger flares, and I can't help the growl in my voice. "Put your hands on me again and I'm out of here. I don't care how much you pay." I shake off his grip, then level a glare at him. "Let's get this over with."

He needs me as much as I need him, so he raises his hands in surrender. "I didn't force you to come."

"Might as well have," I grumble under my breath.

Despite his massive frame, he moves with a lithe grace as he weaves around large metal storage crates that hide a wide open area complete with a boxing ring, free weights, climbing wall, and salmon ladder. "Training for *American Ninja Warrior*?"

"You know as well as I do that you've got to be ready for anything in the field." He jerks a thumb towards the climbing wall. Built that after we lost Paulie a year ago. Dude broke his back trying to scale a three-story building in Kandahar."

"Get ready for mandatory workouts twice a week," a soft-spoken woman with hair the color of rich mahogany says as she rises from a folding chair at the edge of a make-shift kitchen area and then extends a delicate hand. "Inara Ruzgani."

"West. Sampson."

Her slight frame belies the strength of her grip, and her gray eyes don't appear to miss a single detail as she looks me up and down. "Navy man. SEAL?"

"Hooyah," I reply automatically, earning me a slap on the bicep.

"This is Cooper Yarrow," Ryker says, gesturing to the man next to Inara. Cooper mutters his own greeting, then crushes my fingers in a brief handshake. "Coop spent nine years as a flyboy before going private."

Water drips somewhere to my left, and the vague scent of a recent hard workout lingers underneath the aroma of motor oil. No one speaks for several minutes, the other three watching me like they expect me to sprout another head.

"Well," Inara begins as she gestures to the boxing ring, "let's see what you've got."

SWEAT STINGS MY EYES. I swipe the back of my hand over my brows and come away with a streak of blood. Inara rushes forward, driving her shoulder into my solar plexus, but I foil her attempt to knock the wind out of me by grabbing her as I fall back, controlling my descent until I flip her onto her back and land on top of her. Before she can react, I've got my hand around her throat, but she uses my own favorite technique to break my hold, and throws me to the side.

I roll to my feet, and Coop tags in and grabs me. He's stronger than I am, but I maneuver my arm between his legs, hook his thigh, and send him down to the mat.

"How...many times...do I need to beat your asses?" Knees loose, arms slightly raised, I take my defensive stance and wait for one or the other to come at me again.

"Up the wall, Sampson," Ryker orders. "You've got thirty seconds."

You've got to be fucking kidding me. Despite my exhaustion, I vault the ropes surrounding the ring, sprint over to the climbing wall, and take a deep breath as I scan the surface.

"Twenty-six!"

Letting him rattle me isn't an option. One hold, two, three, and I'm climbing. Halfway up, he's put in a trick hold, and the damn thing pops out of the wall, sending me swinging.

"Thirteen seconds, wonder-boy," Coop taunts from below.

"Fuck off." The words escape on a grunt, and I use my momentum to reach a hold three feet to my left. With four seconds to spare, I slap a red square at the top of the wall, and I'm rewarded with a rappelling line dangling in front of me.

Ryker whistles as I land in front of him, then sends me up the salmon ladder. At the top, I dip my hands into a bowl of chalk powder, then leap to a pole to slide back down to the ground, and the three waiting mercenaries staring at me with respect. Ryker extends his hand. "Six years as a civvie hasn't tarnished your skills at all."

"You know what I do for a living. What, exactly, was the point of all this?"

Inara hands me a bottle of water, and I crack the seal as Ryker gestures to a makeshift living room—a couch and two beat-up recliners surrounding a large television—in the far corner of the warehouse. Once we're all seated, the screen flickers to life.

In a dingy room, a bare, yellow bulb spotlights a steel chair bolted to the stained cement floor. Two uniformed officers enter the frame, dragging a thin, bloodied man between them. Once he's tied to the chair with loops of black cord around his wrists, ankles, and chest, one of the officers grabs his greasy black hair and tips his face to the camera.

Holy fuck. "Is that who I think it is?"

"Columbian President Aquliar's son, Ernesto." Ryker meets my gaze, his lips pressed into a thin line. "If we don't get him out in the next seventy-two hours, he's dead. Given the terrain, it's a four-man-op. We're going with or without you, but if you want in, we leave at 0700."

13

CAM

*O*ne solitary desk lamp illuminates the outer office.
Computers sit silent and dark. The scents of coffee and
stale Mountain Dew hang in the air.

I'm numb. Even my headache has faded to a dull memory.
Light spills from Royce's office, and as I raise my hand to rap on
the doorjamb, I have to grit my teeth to stop my fingers from
trembling.

"I heard you the moment you unlocked the front door."
Royce's exhaustion bleeds through his words, and when I find him
slumped in his chair with a glass of bourbon in his hand, I'm
twenty-two again, getting drunk with my CO as we mourn Turk
and Vic—the only two members of our Ordinance Unit ever killed
in the line of duty.

"Have any more of that?"

Royce hands me his glass, then takes a swig from the bottle.
"Lucas called me."

Fuck.

"He quit." After another healthy sip of bourbon, Royce sets the bottle down on the desk. "He'll finish the cabling, but then he's done. Moving back to Lafayette. Starting over somewhere 'without all this baggage.'"

"He…I…" Everything I want to say seems trivial, stupid, useless. Instead, I stare into the glass, focusing on the ripples in the liquid from my trembling fingers. "I'm sorry."

Royce leans forward, his elbows braced on his desk. "Can you fix Oversight in time for LaCosta's party? Be straight with me, Cam. If you can't, say so right now."

I resist the urge to squirm and meet his harsh gaze. "Yes. I'm close. By tomorrow, I'll have stripped out all of the faulty code, and as long as I work my ass off for the next week…"

"I'm assigning Orion as your backup. Use him, Cam. I mean it."

I stifle a cringe, but Royce doesn't seem to notice. Or perhaps he doesn't care.

"Go home. You look like shit. I expect an update by noon tomorrow." He snags the bottle of bourbon again, then turns back to his monitor, dismissing me, and I want to scream at him. If I do, though, all of the frustrations I've kept bottled up for ten years will come pouring out, and I'll end up a blubbering mess on his office floor. No, better to get my ass home where I can fall apart alone.

Without another word, I head for my car.

Are you still there?

Netflix is judging me. I don't know how three episodes of Supernatural passed without me noticing. The remote is heavy and warm in my palm, and when I shut off the television, my stiff fingers have trouble with the buttons, a sign I've been gripping the damn piece of plastic tightly for quite some time.

The clock ticks over to 11:30 p.m., and I check my phone one more time. No messages. I send one more, desperate to talk to

West, to admit all my stupid failings as a programmer, as a friend, and have his arms around me.

Call me, please.

I can't just sit here alone any longer. I'd only picked at my pizza, and my stomach rumbles, even though I don't think I can eat anything.

Except brownies.

Two days, and I haven't been able to get those damn brownies out of my head. So many good memories are tied to those brownies: the rich, chocolaty scent that used to fill the house on Fridays after school, the way Mama would chide Nana for making her gain ten pounds, but would then hug her in the next breath, and vanilla ice cream melting on top of a bowl of warm gooey goodness while Nana told me stories of growing up in Chapala—a small town on the shores of a lake not far from Guadalajara.

I search my memories, tasting the spices she'd add: cinnamon and a pinch of cayenne; seeing two egg yolks in a bowl, ready for me to whisk; and stirring chocolate on the stove until it looked like molten silk.

Before I realize I'm moving, I'm in the car headed for the store. I shop quickly—this late at night the aisles are largely empty—and soon I'm trudging down the hall towards my condo. The bag starts to slip from my grasp as I turn the corner.

West sits next to my door, his arms folded across his knees, head bowed.

"West?" My voice cracks. With care, he gets to his feet, and when I see his face, my stomach flips. Dark shadows brace his eyes, and a small cut over his brow is stark in the fluorescent lights. All night I'd tried to pretend I was okay, but reality crashes down on me as I'm drawn to his side.

He doesn't speak as he slides the grocery bag from my arm so I can unlock my door. Inside, the bag safely on the counter, he slips his arms around me. I can't do much more than sag against his chest, and for a few moments, the pain crushing my heart eases.

"Where were you?" I whisper against his neck.

He stiffens, and I pull away, his reaction taking another chip out of my already fractured heart. I unpack the grocery bag, but as I pull out the eggs, he stops me, his hand cool against my wrist. "Cam, there's so much...I can't stay long—"

"Hand me the mixing bowl?" I gesture to the high shelf in the corner. If I meet his gaze, I won't be able to hold myself together.

He slides the bowl in front of me, and I crack the eggs with one hand, pleased I still remember how. "You don't cook."

"Comfort food. Nana's brownies." I balance myself against the counter as I fish the whisk out of the drawer. I don't even know why I have the damn thing. In six years here, I've never used it.

"Cam, come sit down with me for a few minutes. You look like someone broke your favorite toy. Which is about how I feel."

"I have to get these brownies in the oven." The eggs froth under my vigorous attention, and when they look right, I set the bowl aside so I can add the chocolate to another dish for microwaving. Nana would chide me, but I don't own a double boiler.

"I'm exhausted, angel, and I have to be...somewhere at 5:00 a.m. Take a break. Please." West reaches for my arm, but I take a step back.

"You don't understand. I have to do this right now." Brownies have never been so important. Somewhere deep down, I know I'm being irrational, but I can taste those MREs, feel the baking sun on the back of my neck, hear my crew making fun of me for the lengths I'd go to for those brownies. And then Royce's curt dismissal rings in my ears, and my eyes start to burn.

"You can't give me ten minutes? What the hell happened today that making brownies is more important than—"

My heart threatens to burst from my chest, and the edges of my vision darken as panic takes over. "Nothing else is working! My code is broken, I don't know how I'm going to save the project, my best friend quit today—I've probably lost him forever—and everything hurts. I haven't had these brownies in eighteen years, and I can't even remember the damn recipe!" I turn away from West. As

I reach for the bowl of eggs, I misjudge the distance through the haze of tears, and then the glass tumbles to the tile floor with a sickening crack and a splatter of egg-coated shards.

"Dammit!" More tears threaten, and I try to brace a hand on the counter so I can stoop for the larger pieces, but West drops to his knees and starts piling the remains of the bowl in one hand.

"Hand me that towel." Once he's mopped up most of the liquid, he peers up at me, two of the larger pieces of the bowl balanced in his palm. "Can you call your mother for the recipe?"

"No." I have to force the word out over the lump in my throat as I pull a second, smaller bowl from the cabinet.

After he tosses the broken pieces in the trash, he presses his hand against the small of my back to try to urge me from the kitchen. "Why not?"

The dam breaks, and suddenly I'm shouting. "Because my parents kicked me out when I graduated high school! I haven't spoken to my mother since I woke up in the hospital ten years ago, and the *last* thing I need right now is a lecture on how I ruined my life!"

"I…" He wrestles with his words, the helpless sounds only driving my emotions higher. Pity, shock, and a hint of frustration play across his features, and the fresh egg slips from my fingers to roll across the counter. I track the fall, and as the shell shatters, so do I.

"I don't have birthdays and holidays with cards and flowers and mom's apple pie. My life isn't this neat little package you can wrap into a bow, West. It's messy and complicated, and right now, it just fucking sucks. So don't tell me to 'call my mom' or 'sit down' or 'take a deep breath.' I'm just done."

He doesn't know what to do with me. That's fine. I don't know what to do with myself.

"It's late, and I have to be at work at seven. And I still need to make these damn brownies. I think you should go home."

He stiffens and balls his hands into fists as he closes his eyes, and a muscle in his jaw ticks until he speaks again. "Look, I'll help you with the brownies. You're upset, and I'm worried you're going to hurt yourself."

My walls rise, higher and stronger than ever before, and despite the urge to cut West a door so he can join me on the other side, I can only offer him a cold stare.

"I can take care of myself. Been doing it for a long time. I don't need your help."

We face off with a broken egg and pieces of glass between us, the scent of chocolate perfuming the air. He breaks first, and as his shoulders slump and he shoves a hand into his pocket, I'm not sure if I've won or lost.

"I thought—" He runs his free hand through his hair. "Never mind." Then he turns on his heel. As he yanks open my door, he tosses a glance over his shoulder. "I won't be around for a while, Cam. Just thought you should know."

The door slams, and I stare at the remnants of my feeble attempt at comfort. I'm spent. I couldn't muster a tear now if I shoved half an onion directly into my eyes, despite the shame I feel. With a groan, I lower myself to the floor so I can clean up my mess. Well, one of them. The fractured pieces of my soul might be beyond fixing.

14

WEST

*T*he drone of the plane's engines—along with the stress and anticipation that kept me up all night—lull me into a Zen state. Neither asleep nor awake, I hover on the edge of consciousness, Cam's last words on repeat.

"I can take care of myself. Been doing it for a long time. I don't need your help."

Fuck those goddamn brownies.

"You ready for this?" Ryker's booming voice through my headset jars me awake, and my heart stutters before I get my breathing under control. He peers down at me, a hand steadying himself on one of the plane's support struts. "You look like shit."

"Whose fault is that?" I gesture to the bruise above my right eye. Despite my training, Inara got a couple of good jabs in, and my knuckles still ache from the impact with Coop's back. "You've seen me on mission. Once we hit the ground, I'll be good."

A shadow passes over Ryker's scarred cheek. "Never saw anyone focus the way you do, Sampson. Analyze the situation for weak points, execute a plan without a single fault. I owe you my life."

I meet his dark gaze. "All part of the job. Pretty sure you saved my ass out there too." After a quick glance at my watch and altimeter, I shove to my feet. "You're sure your intel's solid?"

"Ernesto's in the center of a ten acre compound. Eleven total men, five highly trained, the rest grunts. My contact tells me they'll make another video at 14:00. If we don't get him before they transfer him from his cell to the interrogation room, our chances of him making it out in one piece go down dramatically." Ryker offers me a tablet, but I wave it away.

"I studied the layout all night. I'm good."

"You better be." Inara straps her ammo pack to her left thigh. The diminutive sharpshooter carries her kills in the depths of her brown eyes. All business, her hair tightly braided under her helmet, she checks her own wrist unit. "Five minutes to drop."

As I stagger to the back of the plane where the bay doors reveal nothing but open sky over what feels like an endless ocean, I remember the way Cam's fingers stroked down my chest, her arms around me as I woke in the throes of a nightmare, her laughter as we decimated a horde of foes in *Gears of War*.

When I'm back, when lives don't depend on my every move, we'll finish that fight, and then I'll walk away. My heart seizes as I imagine life without her. *Focus, Sampson. Put it away. She doesn't want you.* I squeeze my eyes shut as I picture the drop zone. The plane banks, and when I pull down my goggles and let myself see once more, she's gone, only the mission in front of me.

CAM

Crumbs from the world's worst brownie litter my desk. You'd think after West slammed the door last night, I'd have abandoned my obsession with the damn recipe and gone after him. You'd be wrong.

Shame—at losing my shit, at failing Lucas, at driving away three people in less than a week—kept me frozen for too long, and then I slipped on the puddle of egg and went down hard. My right butt cheek is four shades of purple now, and I broke down and took a rare morning Vicodin. Sitting in my chair is pure torture, but what choice do I have?

"You're here early."

Royce's deep voice startles me, and I drop the dusty, chocolate brick, sending more detritus onto my desk. "Dammit." As I turn the keyboard upside down and shake it, Royce heads for the coffee machine.

"You're not actually drinking *office* coffee, are you?" He holds the half-full pot aloft. I meet his gaze, and his eyes widen. "What happened?"

Great. So I *do* look as terrible as I feel. "You mean besides Lucas quitting and *something* fucking up the code so we almost lose the Coana job? Isn't that enough for one week?" I clench my hands into fists as the tension holding my head in a vise squeezes harder. "I've got to check every one of the subroutines to make sure what-ever happened didn't cause any other issues, and Oversight is still crashing every time I try to load the biometric module."

Royce takes a step back in surrender. "Orion will be here in an hour. Put him to work."

I shove an unruly curl behind my ear. "He's never touched Oversight's code, and he's not certified in Python yet. He can analyze the performance monitors, but the rest? It's all on me. The success of this whole damn project, of everything I've worked for this past year, it's all my responsibility. You want to help me? Leave me the hell alone." *Because you're so damn good at it* remains unsaid.

We stare at one another until he sighs and returns his focus to his coffee, and suddenly I'm back in the hospital, my leg immobi-lized with rods and pins sticking out at all angles, two surgeries in, with another six ahead of me. *Stop. Don't go,* my wounded soul screams. But the only words I can force out barely make any sense. "Can you even see me?"

His shoulders hike up to his ears as he sets the sugar container back on the counter and then takes a long time stirring his coffee. When he sets the spoon aside, a weariness stiffens his movements.

"I see you." Royce brings me a fresh cup of coffee as a peace offering. "I'm trying to help you." When he rests a hand on my shoulder, I'm tempted to lean in, but my anger flares.

"'Help me'? You're working so damn hard because you can't stand to look at me. To see what happened to me and *deal* with it. I got hurt, Royce. No one's to blame, but I still spent a year in the hospital and rehab, and another nine months before I could do much more than stand up without assistance. I don't need your help. I got by without it when things were a hell of a lot harder than they are right now. So go hide in your office and continue to ignore me. It's what you're best at, after all."

When did I start crying? The air conditioner cools the wet tracks on my cheeks, and I swipe at the offending tears with as much anger as I can muster. Until Royce flees to his office. The door slams, and I'm back in my kitchen as West walked out on me.

With no one around, I let myself break. The sobs start as I sink into my chair, then turn to hiccups after the fourth tissue. I sound like someone's strangling a frog, and the thought helps me claw my way up from the pit of overwhelming emotion I've fallen into.

The brownie is now a salty mess, tears turning the chocolate into—well, something that resembles a kid's mud pie. The scent of Aqua Velva from my first ever boyfriend wraps around me, and I'm sitting at the counter in my parents' kitchen with Mama's arm around me, my teenage sobs ruining another brownie—this one made with love and care.

"Stop it." I pinch my arm as hard as I can, using the pain to focus until my breathing returns to normal. Luckily, no one else chose to show up early today so I can take a few minutes to compose myself. My little makeup bag saves me, and soon, other than my red-rimmed and puffy eyes, you'd never know anything was wrong.

Bringing up Oversight's control panel, I give the computer my sternest glare. "You are going to behave, or I'll dismantle you line by line until you're begging for mercy."

BY THE END of the day, I'm ready to throw my computer off a tall building and move to a tropical island with no internet access. I could work as a bartender at a cushy resort. Somewhere no one knows my history, and I can start over. Somewhere I'll never see Lucas, Royce, or West again.

At least Oversight appears stable. I haven't found a single bug in the past four hours, and when I sent Orion over to the Coana Hotel to upload her new code, the system hummed along perfectly.

As I sweep my sandwich wrapper and soda cup into the trash, my eyes start to water again. My silent phone taunts me. A dozen times today, I tried to find the words to reach out to West, but how do you apologize for completely irrational behavior? I couldn't even manage to give him a coherent answer to why making those brownies was so damn important.

Royce's door bangs open, and he fills the narrow space as he scans the office. I'm the only one left, and I know for damn sure he doesn't want to talk to me. The feeling's mutual.

"Have you moved at all today?" His weary voice startles me, and I choke on my seven hundredth cup of coffee. "I didn't think so. Come on."

As I get to my feet, the bruise from last night's fall sends an intense wave of pain down my leg. Royce stops a few steps away, concern furrowing his brow until I wave him off. "I'm fine. Where are we—?"

With a quick flash of his palm, he shows me the pack of cigarettes, then leads me out into the alley. There's nowhere to sit here, so I lean against the brick wall of the building while he lights up. The rich scent of cloves and tobacco stirs the memory of my grandfather's favorite brand. Not exactly the same, but close enough.

When he offers me a puff, I can't help myself. I haven't smoked since I got out of the army, and I take a long, slow pull, rolling the smoke around on my tongue. Out here in the fresh air, I can pretend no time has passed, and we're at the PX stocking up on gum and caffeine pills.

Wispy clouds paint the sky with practiced strokes, and when I glance back to find him watching me, I'm surprised at the sorrow I find in his eyes.

"About earlier…"

"Oversight is stable. Orion's hanging out at Coana for the next few hours to keep an eye on the performance monitors. We'll be fine."

"I didn't doubt you." He takes a drag on his cigarette and then exhales with a heavy sigh. "What happened between us?"

The question throws me, and I stammer a few unintelligible half-words before I manage to put a coherent thought together. "I got blown up, and you disappeared."

He frowns and starts to reply, but this might be my only chance to say all the things I've wanted to say for ten years.

"I needed you, Royce. Do you have any idea what it was like to wake up in a hospital bed alone with three broken ribs, a punctured lung, nine shattered bones in my hip, leg, and arm, burns, a concussion, and internal bleeding?" As he hangs his head, I continue. "You were the first person I asked for. I could barely speak after having a tube down my throat for two days. After a week, the nurses were sick of me. They'd bring me a meal, and they'd say, 'No, Camilla, no one's heard from him.' Everyone else visited. Bonzo and Yankov took shifts by my bedside when the doctors had to put me in a medically-induced coma for a week. Bucky let me cry all over him when they warned me I might lose my leg. Where were you?"

He drops the cigarette on the pavement and grinds the ball of his foot against the smoldering stub. "I took another commission."

"No shit. Why? The army wouldn't have forced that on you. Not right away. You could have come. Even once." My voice cracks, and I clench my free hand, digging my nails into my palm as hard as I can. "I didn't hear from you for almost five years. Five years! And then you show up and offer me a job? I was so fucking pissed at you, I almost slammed the door in your face. But I hoped working for you would give us a chance to rebuild our friendship. I should have known better."

His fingers shake as he withdraws another cigarette, and after the fourth failed attempt at working the lighter, I hold out my hand. We're so close I can smell his aftershave, but the second I squelch the flame, he starts to pace. "I failed you, Cam. Hell, I failed the whole team. I didn't see the debris around you. Yankov tried to warn me. He'd seen a similar setup with his last team. I ignored him. If I hadn't, if we hadn't all gone out drinking the night before, if Bravo team's disposal specialist hadn't come down with food poisoning, you'd be able to walk without that damn cane."

"Playing 'what if' won't get you anywhere." I pause until he meets my gaze. "I never blamed you. I chose this life, Royce. I could have gone into cyber ops, but diffusing bombs was challenging and dangerous and thrilling. I knew the risks. Eighty-six times I cheated death. Eighty-six times I had your voice in my ear keeping me calm. How could you just abandon me when I needed you most?" The dam I built over the past ten years crumbles, and the full torrent of my emotions washes over me. "You were my brother, and when you disappeared, you took away the only family I had left."

The crash as he kicks a dumpster sends my heart rate soaring, and I must make some sound because he whirls around. Remorse presses down on his shoulders.

"I'm sorry. I'm so sorry." His chest stutters as he draws in a breath. "I couldn't bear to see you broken by my mistakes. I didn't know staying away would make things worse."

Blinking up at the sky to try to stop my tears from spilling over, I choose my next words carefully. "I survived, Royce."

"Did you?" He takes my hand, his fingers warm and rough. "I've never seen you lose control. Ever. Not in the worst firefight. Not when we lost Tommy. The past few days..."

Now I'm the one pulling back. "I can't. Not...yet."

"Cam."

His "big brother" tone grates, even though it's one of the things I've missed most about him. "A lot's happened in ten years. This week—the past couple of days—life has seemed determined to kick me in the ass every chance it gets. Can we leave it at that for now?"

I ache all over, but in my heart most of all. I want to run, but I force myself to meet his gaze. My friend, my only family, shakes his head slowly.

"I wish we could. But Cam...I'm sick."

The world falls away from underneath me, but before I hit the ground, his arm wraps around my waist, and he steadies me until I find my footing again.

His thin frame—so obvious as I lean against him—should have clued me in, but I've been wrapped up in my own shit for so long, I couldn't see past the chasm between us. "Explain," I manage as I brace hand against his chest.

"My second commission." He stares up at the sky, as if he's trying to decide how much to tell me. I extricate myself from his grip, trying to give him space to tell me what he needs. He starts to pace slowly. "I refused to command another ordinance crew, and I hated myself so much, I went to my CO and demanded he find the riskiest missions he could—the ones no one else wanted." Royce's voice falters. "I wanted to die serving my country, not live out my days knowing I'd failed my team."

My cheeks are wet again, and I swipe at the offending tears. "You didn't—"

"Let me finish. Please." His third cigarette seems to calm him, though he only takes three puffs before he tosses it away. "There's no proof. But, I spent months disposing of sarin gas and depleted uranium. We took precautions—shit, more precautions than you could ever imagine. But..."

"Royce."

He meets my gaze. "There's a golf-ball-sized tumor pressing down on my brain stem. Docs aren't sure if it's cancer or not. With surgery, I've got a thirty percent chance of a normal life. Without... the doctors give me two months."

Our entire friendship plays on fast-forward. How intimidated I was when I met him. How I found him drunk off his ass behind the mess two weeks later, hung up on some girl back home. How he reamed me for not double-checking my suit on my first solo disposal. How wrecked I was the night I told him why my parents don't speak to me anymore.

"You're having the surgery. Please tell me you're having the surgery." If he says no, I don't know how I'll stay upright.

"In ten days." He clears his throat, and at his sides, his fists tremble slightly. "I can't do this without you, Pint."

My long-ago nickname, Pint-Sized—because despite my height, I was thin as a rail when I joined the army—sends me over the edge, and I wrap my arms around him as we cling to all we each have left. Each other.

I can't sleep. After spending an hour with Dr. Google researching brain stem tumors, I'm terrified for Royce. He wants me to take over the company while he recovers, but what do I know about managing people? I can't even open up to my boyfriend—former boyfriend, I guess, as he hasn't contacted me. I sent him an "are you there?" message, but he hasn't responded, so I give up and pour myself a generous shot of bourbon as I log on to VetNet.

More than once I switch over to the chat window, wishing I

could talk to West, but he's been offline for three days now. As my eyes start to burn again, I click on HuskyFan's name.

He read my last message as soon as I sent it, and he posted on the Vents and Rants board yesterday about his mother-in-law and how his second job presented an unexpected challenge when he had to outsmart a particularly ugly problem, but he hasn't replied to me.

"What the hell?" Maybe today's my day for things to work out. After all, I managed an honest conversation with Royce, despite the pain it caused. Seems safe enough to test the waters with a guy I've never met in person.

FlashPoint: *Hey, HF. I haven't heard from you in a few days. Life... hasn't been great here. I think I broke up with my guy, and work sucks ass. One of my coworkers—a friend—quit, and I'm afraid he'll never forgive me. My boss...well, we talked and we might be almost solid again, but he's got some serious shit going on and I'm worried about him. I hope you're doing better. Having fun at your side job? Is that helping things with your wife any? Check in, okay? I could really use a friend right now, and they seem to be in short supply these days.*

After I brush my teeth, I return to my laptop to see that he's read the message, but again, hasn't replied. Maybe my luck hasn't changed that much after all.

15

CAM

*a*s I've chipped away at Oversight's last remaining problems the past three days, my own have percolated in the background. Coming face-to-face with my failings in the long hours I've spent alone in front of a computer has left me questioning everything, and I don't like the answers I've found. Give me a bomb and I know what to do. Wires, circuits, timers, and fuel all behave in logical, predictable ways. Put me in front of a man I care deeply for—a man I might even have been able to love—and I'm paralyzed with fear.

I've spent a good portion of my nights thinking about our time together. West shared his life with me. Not just the pretty parts, but the uncomfortable, messy bits that no one likes to acknowledge: his nightmares, his business troubles, his perceived failings as a SEAL team leader.

What did I do? I pushed him away rather than admit my own shortfalls as a friend, a programmer, a partner. When I can breathe again, I'll show up at his door and apologize in person. Even if we can't find our way back to a relationship, he deserves that much.

For what I hope is the final time before we turn the system on for good, I update the Oversight server. One module, two, three, four...I hold my breath as I watch the system monitor after each piece of the software comes online. No memory leaks. I shudder as a small piece of stress falls away. Finally. "You beautiful piece of ones and zeroes. I want to kiss you!" If I could dance, I'd pick up the laptop and waltz around the room. Instead, I settle for blowing a kiss at the screen with an exaggerated *"mwah!"*

"Would you like to be alone?" Royce slips through the door into Coana's server room with a cappuccino in his hand. "This is a hotel. I'm pretty sure you could rent a room and go at it with the software all night long."

I throw a wadded-up Post-It note at him, but my aim sucks, and the projectile bounces off the to-go cup seconds before he hands me the steaming beverage.

"You're a god." The rich, caffeinated nectar revives me, and I close my eyes to enjoy the sensation.

"How are you doing?" He's largely left me alone this week, but the few times we've found ourselves in the same room, he's been more like the old Royce, the one who knew me back when I barely knew myself. He won't talk about his upcoming surgery—not in any detail—but his voice carries a near permanent sadness that I ache to be able to ease.

I should tell him the truth. Should tell him how every night I go home and have to talk myself out of reaching for the bourbon to quiet my demons. How I miss West. How I both dread going to Coana and wish I could spend every minute here because I hate being alone in a condo that still smells vaguely of chocolate.

Instead, I force a half-smile. Avoidance, on sale now. Fifty percent off with a bonus free gift of cowardice. If I stick my head in the sand, the rest of the world will go away, right? He peers down at me, concern drawing a single line between his brows. Bags bruise the pale skin under his eyes.

My own issues beat a hasty retreat in the face of a man who

might not see next month. "I'm fine. I'm more worried about you. Sit down. What did the doctor say?"

A weary groan escapes as he settles into the chair next to mine. "Which one? I've got doctor's appointments every day. MRIs, CAT scans, therapy—I might as well move in to Harborview Medical Center now. I hear the rent's somewhere north of outrageous, though."

I struggle not to roll my eyes or berate him for his humor. "What do you need for post-op care?"

"My brother will come up if I make it through the surgery." He stares at his hands clasped around the coffee cup in his lap. "I told him not to book anything until they know. He's got two kids, his wife works full time...he doesn't need to waste his vacation unless there's a good chance I'm going to be...me at the end of this whole thing."

"I'll be there for the surgery. For as long as you need me."

Shock paints his drawn features with a pinkish hue, and he shakes his head. "Don't."

"Why the hell not?" I barely recognize my own voice, indignation, worry, and desperation mixing to thicken my words. "You're my only family, Rolls. There's nothing you can do to stop me."

His eyes water, and damn if a tear doesn't race down his stubbled cheek. We both look away, unwilling to own up to our own weaknesses, but I reach out and squeeze his hand, and he holds on for a few seconds before he clears his throat and pulls away.

Glancing down at his watch, he scowls. "LaCosta's waiting for me. We're good to go, right?"

For the first time in more than a week, my response doesn't come full of wishful thinking. "Oversight is ready. The network resources are still a little higher than I'd like, but nothing the system can't handle. I think I've finally eliminated the last of the corrupted code. As of ten minutes ago, the entire system's operational."

Relief lightens his expression, and a genuine smile —one I haven't witnessed in more than ten years—deepens the lines around his eyes. I can still see him as he was in Afghanistan. Thirty-eight and full of fire, he didn't let anyone or anything stand in his way. Now, the reality of his years and his illness sinks in, and I can't ignore the gray mixed in with the sandy brown at his temples or the tremble in his arms as he pushes to his feet.

"Great. Hang out until I'm done meeting with him then have a drink with me?"

New Royce isn't doing much for my equilibrium, despite how much I wanted my friend back. I twist my messy curls into a bun so I can secure them away from my face, giving me a moment to process this shift. I've been looking forward to my recliner and a couple of episodes of *Supernatural* all day, but I can't say no. Not when I might not have many more chances.

"Sure. Just one, though. I haven't managed to get to bed before 2:00 a.m. all week, and I'm wiped."

"Just one." He laughs, as if the idea of us stopping at a single drink is the best joke he's heard all day, and then yanks open the door. As I return my attention to the screens showing the feeds from our cameras, my heart stops.

The hallway outside the server room is empty, yet I know Royce is only steps away from the door. Five seconds. Seven. Ten. Why the hell don't I see him on screen? At twelve seconds, Royce emerges.

Fuck, fuck, fuck. Pushing to my feet, I groan as my hip screams a sharp protest. Ignoring the throbbing pain, I throw open the door and try for a pathetic run, but the elevator doors shut before I can get more than a few feet down the hall.

I try to call, and when I'm shuttled off to his voice mail, I send him an emergency text, then head back to the server room. Once there, I dig into my bag of tricks—shallow as it is—to try to trace the traffic from Oversight to the internet. That's next-level-hacker shit, though, and all I can tell is that a highly compressed data stream is leaving the hotel for parts unknown. "Son of a bitch. What the fuck is going on?"

Running system diagnostics doesn't return anything useful.

"Dammit. Why won't you talk to me?" Oversight hums along, oblivious to my pleas, and I'm about to try blatant threats when Royce shoves the door open hard enough to rattle the server racks. "What's wrong?"

My heart pounds as I meet his gaze. "Someone's sending Oversight's data outside the hotel. They might be watching our every move."

What little color he has drains, and he takes my arm to help me up. "We've got to tell LaCosta. Now."

"Not until I shut the system down."

As I go through the controlled shutdown procedure, Royce's expression mirrors my hopelessness. All the crap that I've dealt with the past two weeks comes down to this. The network traffic spikes make perfect sense now. All those extra lines of code, every single corrupted function.

"How could this happen?" He gives voice to the question on my lips, and I shake my head.

"I don't know, but this isn't just corrupted code, Royce. This is sabotage."

"Sit," Phillip says with a smile. "How soon can you turn on Oversight?"

With a quick glance at Royce, I fold my hands in my lap to stop fidgeting. "We can't." I explain what's happening—at least what I understand of it—as Phillip's face pales.

"C-can you tell who did this? Where the data's...um...going?"

If the man thinks much harder, I'll hear the wheels turning. "No. I tried a quick packet trace, but someone sophisticated enough to hack my code wouldn't leave their data unencrypted. They're probably bouncing the signal to hell and back with two dozen different points in between. I'm good at what I do, Phillip, but this is next level shi—err, stuff. You'd need a true hacker or maybe the NSA.

145

"What I can do," I shift slightly to relieve a deep ache in my hip, "is pull every programmer we have off their other assignments and analyze the code line by line. We'll lock these bastards out for good before we turn Oversight on."

When I chance a quick look at Royce, he offers me an almost imperceptible nod of approval as he hands me his iPad. I'm not ready. Not like this. Not…without knowing if he'll be around to see this job to its conclusion.

He saves me from my momentary panic. "You'll have to keep your old system running a little longer. Cam, how long do you need?"

"Five d-days should do it, but I'd like fourteen to be safe." Thankful he has my back, yet terrified that Royce is going to be in a hospital bed for a large portion of this time, I try to force some confidence into my voice. "I've been chasing these hackers for two weeks now, I just didn't know it. But that means I have their signature—code is a lot like handwriting in some ways. My team can stop them."

"I can't believe this is happening again," Phillip mutters, half to himself. He drops his head into his hands and stares down at his desk blotter.

"Again?" Royce leans forward, bracing his hands on the edge of the desk. "What the hell do you mean 'again'?"

Phillip sighs. "Six months ago, the Seattle PD ran a major drug sting across all of the downtown hotels. Apex Hotel—right across the street—yielded the most arrests. They nabbed three young men in business suites carrying suitcases full of heroin and cocaine."

"In downtown Seattle?" I can't help the shock in my voice.

"Hotels are the perfect places to sell drugs," Phillip explains. "All the guests in and out? No one's going to notice a well-dressed man or woman carrying a suitcase or duffel bag. The police tried to arrest a suspect here, but he got off." Frustration etches deep lines in Phillip's face, and I feel for the man. "The kid managed to dump the drugs in a trash can before the police arrested him, and when they scanned the security camera footage, they discovered that our cameras didn't capture a single image of him past the main lobby. He headed for the back of the hotel, but as soon as he moved into the hall leading to the pool, the system lost him."

"You don't have that many blind spots." Understanding washes over me, and I try not lose my temper in front of the client. "Someone tampered with the old system too, didn't they?"

"I don't know. Or didn't. Not until just now. The system's buggy. Always has been. Unexplained outages every few weeks, flickering images, the occasional alarm going off for no reason. My facilities manager installed a relay switch on a timer to cycle the power every day. That helped until last year. Around 6:00 p.m. most days, the cameras blink. Just for a minute or two."

"What did your facilities manager say?" If his clipped tone is any indicator, Royce is as angry as I am. "And what about the guys who installed your current system?"

"Kyle was terminated right after the raid. He disappeared on a bender for two days. Brickyard Security claimed their system was flawless and our camera problem was operator error. That's when I called you."

Puzzle pieces are rotating and snapping into place inside my head. Relays, the non-standard wiring, the hassles installing the card reader module and HVAC controls...I'm so caught up in my own thoughts, I must not hear Royce calling my name, because he touches my arm, then asks if I'm all right.

"I've got to get back to the office—and I need Lucas to come with me. I can't explain anymore right now, but give me a couple of hours and I'll have some answers for you."

"Go," Royce says with a terse nod. "I'll meet you back there in an hour."

16

CAM

*O*n the nineteenth floor, I freeze outside the doors to the electrical closet. The seconds tick by, turning a brief pause into an awkward "what the hell are you doing?" interlude. In the end, fate takes over. One of the cabling crew—Zach, I think— bursts out of the room and almost runs me down. "Sorry, ma'am," he mutters as he hurries down the hall.

Lucas, stooped on the floor with a cable cutter in his hands, glances up, and his half-grin fades.

"Can I talk to you?" I can't force my voice much above a whisper.

"You're the boss." With a shrug and those three words, he cuts me deep, and I try not to let the bleeding show.

I step into the room and glance around. The old cameras never covered this room, and the new camera is clutched in Lucas's hand. "Where's everyone else?"

"On twenty. This is the last camera on this floor." He sets the tiny device on a cart and then shoves his hands into his pockets.

"What do you want? If I don't get distracted, I can finish this job today and be done with Seattle."

I reach for his arm, but he pulls away. "Please. I'm an ass. I... I'm sorry. I never meant to shut you out. I just...don't know how to need anyone."

"You don't *want* to need anyone, honey. Somehow you got the idea that means you're strong. That's not what strength is. Strength is asking for help when you're in over your head. You keep shutting people out, you're going to end up alone."

"I know." I refuse to let myself look away from his disapproving gaze, even though I feel about an inch tall right now. "Did you know Royce was sick?"

"Yes." Lucas's expression softens. "I swear, the two of you are so alike it's creepy. Both too proud and stubborn to reach out. I went to him when you started staying up all night debugging and refused my help. We got to talking. He didn't want to die without knowing you'd be okay, but he was too scared to approach you. If you'd blown him off, I think it would have broken him."

Despite the repairs Royce and I have made to our friendship the past few days, Lucas's words sting, and I blink back tears. "I got so caught up in trying to fix Oversight, I couldn't see my way clear. Please, Lucas. Give me another chance. I need you with me at Emerald City. I'm not Wonder Woman."

"No. But you could pull off the costume." He tries for a grin and I can't help my half-laugh/half-sob. As he drapes his arm over my shoulder and pulls me in for a quick hug, his chest heaves. "I can't stay. I'll never work anywhere else in this town. TechLock all but confirmed that."

"Work with me." Drawing back, I clutch his forearms. "Please. If I'm going to run Emerald City for a few months, I need the best programmer around handling ZoomWare. I saw some of the subroutines you wrote for the biometrics and card control modules. They were fucking brilliant. The whole HVAC module was pure genius."

"I'll cop to the HVAC and biometrics work, but I didn't write anything for card control."

Fuck. The puzzle in my head coalesces as the missing piece lands right in front of me. "That's how they got in."

"What?" He cocks his head. "Who?"

"All the problems with Oversight the past few weeks? Someone hacked her, and I think I just figured out how they did it." Praying harder than I've prayed in a long time, I hold out my hand. "Help me fix her."

Indecision holds him still as he searches my gaze. "If I do, we're a team. No more Wonder Woman shit."

"The only Wonder Woman shit you'll see is her logo on my coffee mug."

As Lucas shakes my hand, a small piece of my world rights itself once more. My momentary jubilation fades as my thoughts travel unbidden to West. If only righting that ship were this simple.

Two hours later, Royce carries boxes of pizza into the conference room while I hook my laptop up to the projection screen. Orion and Abby huddle around Lucas as he flags line after line of code we need to strip out of the card control module.

"How do you *see* all that, man?" Orion says as Lucas highlights a whole function that needs to go.

"Easy." He glances up at me and winks. "Cam's got a signature. You work with someone long enough, you learn their tells."

"Which is why I never play poker with him," I add as I snag a slice of pepperoni.

Orion rubs his bald head. "Yeah, but you said you never worked on this module. I don't see any difference between those two functions."

As Lucas throws my code and the hacker's side-by-side and

launches into a detailed comparison, Royce offers me a cold beer. "How are we looking?"

"Better than I expected. With their help, Oversight's code could be pristine by tomorrow. Then we just need to figure out how to keep her that way." The crisp lager soothes my nerves, though despite my outward confidence, I have no idea how the hacker accessed the code in the first place.

"Hey, Lucas?" Al leans against the conference room door jamb, his Mariner's ball cap half-crushed in his hands. "What's the schedule for tomorrow?"

Lucas pushes back from the table and motions for me and Al to follow him out of the conference room. I give him a subtle nod when he looks to me for approval and let him lead—both physically and professionally.

"Cam found a glitch in Oversight. Until we fix the code, she needs me here. Can you direct the crew tomorrow on twenty and the rooftop deck?"

"Yeah." Al runs his fingers through his short-cropped hair, and a tattoo peeks out from his sleeve.

"I didn't know you'd served." I shrug off my sweater and show him my unit's tattoo. "What'd you do?"

"Radar. Not something I like to talk about." He presses his lips together, tugs his sleeve down, then glances back into the conference room. "That must be some epic glitch."

"You have no idea." I rub the back of my neck. "We're damn lucky the system didn't go live like this. Once we're done, though, no one will ever touch her again."

A LITTLE PAST TEN, I interrupt everyone. "Go home. We can finish cleaning up the code tomorrow. Show up with any and all ideas to make sure whoever fucked with Oversight can't touch her again."

Abby, Orion, and Royce take off, but Lucas hoofs the pizza boxes and beer bottles out to the dumpster while I copy all of

Oversight's code onto an encrypted flash drive, then secure the drive in the office safe.

Picking up my laptop bag, I meet his gaze. "Have a drink with me?" I don't want to go home, and while we're solid enough for him to help debug Oversight, I don't yet know if he'll stay once the project is done. He hasn't been his usual animated self this evening, and I'm worried about him.

We end up at ZigZag, one of the quieter—and better—bars in the city. Over glasses of Irish whiskey, we try to figure out how the hacker gained access to Oversight in the first place.

"LaCosta sent all of the old system's camera footage from the past week to SPD this afternoon. The hacker had to access Oversight from Coana's server room. We've had our card reader module on that door all week, though, and the only people swiping in and out were you and me, Coana's head of security, their IT manager, and Royce."

Lucas sits back in his chair, the glass of whiskey cupped in his large hands. "What do you know about the guys Al brought in to help with the cabling?"

The whiskey warms me, and I roll my head from side-to-side. "Nothing. Royce handled all of that. Why?"

After a sigh, Lucas drains his glass, then motions to the server for another round. "I was pretty messed up when I got kicked out of the army. My mama couldn't work anymore, and I needed to make some fast cash to pay for her health insurance. When I fell in with the Guild Crew down in Los Angeles, all my money woes disappeared. They used the hotels, too."

"You don't talk about that time much."

"One of these days, honey, we're going to get smashed and then there won't be any more secrets between us." He toasts me, though his words still sting. "A couple of days ago, I couldn't find my keycard when we moved from sixteen to seventeen. Al told me to go on ahead and he'd have Zach check the crawlspaces."

"You think…"

"Al said Zach found my card outside the service elevator."

Lucas stares into his second whiskey. "I was so pissed at you that afternoon. TechLock had just laughed in my face. I took the damn card out of my wallet and almost snapped it in half. But I swear I put it back."

"You think they might have used it. To do what? Even with access to the server room, they wouldn't be able to hack Oversight's encryption."

"I know." He drums his fingers on the table. "But, Cam, this is Seattle. The land of Microsoft. Google. How hard would it be to find someone?"

"I'll issue all new keycard codes tomorrow. If they did use your card—even if they cloned the damn thing—we'll lock them out. Beyond that...I hope the police can find something on those tapes."

The server drops the check on the table with a smile, and Lucas narrows his eyes at me.

"You haven't said a single word about your SEAL all night. Haven't checked your phone once." He sits back with a sigh. "What happened?"

"Same shit, different day." Lucas's arched brow has me withering. "We had a fight, and I kicked him out. I'm pretty sure he's done with my drama. Refusing to listen to your boyfriend when he's upset because you're too caught up in your own problems doesn't make for good partner material."

"Have you tried calling him?"

"No." I already know what Lucas is going to say, but I still stare at the floor when he chastises me.

"You're an epic failure in the apology department. You know that, right? Give me your phone." Resting his hand palm up on the table, he cocks his head.

Bossy Lucas usually makes me laugh, then give in to his demands, but I can't let someone else bail me out this time. "No. If West and I have a chance, I have to fix things myself. After I finish this job."

"Nuh-uh. Now. We're not leaving until you apologize to the

man. You want to tell that poor bartender over there she's got to stay past closing?" Crossing his arms, he settles deeper into the leather captain's chair. "Go outside and call him right now."

"Fine." I snap the response, but inside, I'm terrified. Dealing with all of my failings in just a few days doesn't leave much protection around my heart.

Only a few tourists wander the waterfront this time of night, and I huddle under one of the bar's tall outdoor heaters as I wait for West to answer. My heart races until I hear his voice mail message. I almost hang up, but I'm not fast enough—maybe because I don't want to be, and when I hear the beep, I don't even think.

"I've played the other night on repeat in my head all week. You asked me for ten minutes, and I refused. I don't have an excuse. I was scared, but you deserve better than a woman who can't get past her own problems to see that her partner needs her." My voice cracks and the lump in my throat threatens to choke me, but I have to finish this. "I'm sorry. For losing my shit, for ignoring your pain, for not showing you just how much I care. For not letting you in. I...I'm damn close to falling in love with you, West. Please call me back."

As I hang up, a star streaks across the sky, and I wipe away a single tear as I make my wish. If only I had better luck with silly little children's rituals.

"I left a voice mail," I tell Lucas as I reach our table.

"That's a start." He unfolds his tall frame from the chair and tries to stifle a yawn. "You're the strongest person I know, Cam. Don't let fear steal a chance for real happiness."

No amount of rehearsal is going to make my next words any easier, so once we're outside, I rush before I lose my nerve.

"Not many people are lucky enough to work with their best friend. I did a damn good job of screwing that up, and you still came back and helped me fix Oversight. Please think about staying on after we finish this project. I'll understand if you don't, but...I need you."

He offers me a firm embrace, and in his arms, I find a sliver of forgiveness. We part ways, and I'm so wiped, I don't notice until I crawl into bed that West never called me back.

WEST

Retired from active duty for six years and not much has changed. Ryker distributes rations, and the four of us crouch against a low hill as we chow down on something that resembles meatloaf—if you close your eyes, don't inhale, and swallow quickly. At least the comms are more comfortable.

"Now that El Presidente has refused to pay Ernesto's ransom, the guerrillas want a show," Ryker says as he lays the ruggedized tablet on the damp forest litter between us. On screen, the leader of the extremist group known only as the People's Army pulls Ernesto's head back by his hair, then rests a machete against his carotid artery.

"Your president cares little for anyone but himself. He will not save his own son. How can you ever trust him to save you? At midnight, we will take his son's life, but his is not the first blood spilled in this war. Your brothers, sisters, mothers, and fathers, daughters, and sons have died so your beloved leader can have his gilded cage. To that we say, 'No more.'"

The hostage screams as the madman flicks the machete upwards and slices into Ernesto's bruised and swollen cheek. The camera zooms in on his frightened and probably drug-addled stare, and then the video fades to black.

"Rewind twenty seconds." Unlike the others, I've watched this video—and the four others the People's Army released—a dozen times, looking for any intel that will make our infiltration and subsequent escape easier.

Ryker taps the screen, then hands me the tablet. Playing the same five seconds over and over again while the others wait, silent, I take in every detail of the room. A dirty window high on the wall provides the only natural light, and shadows flicker twice as the machete-wielding asshole talks about first blood. One of the other guerrillas in the room stifles a flinch, and a third casts a quick glance upwards.

"They moved him." I zoom in on the window. "The angle of the sun is all wrong. Our current breach plan won't work."

"Fuck." Ryker glares at Coop. "If you hadn't gotten your chute stuck in that tree, we'd be home by now."

Coop holds up his hands. "I don't control the wind, man. The plan's solid. Why do we have to change it?"

"Shut up." Inara, who claims the *Firefly* character of the same name was named after her and not the other way around, punches Coop in the arm. "We brought Sampson in to handle shit like this. Let him do his job."

"Give me an hour." Creeping off to a deeper depression in the mossy landscape, I visualize the layout of the compound. Keeping this team safe is my mission, and I can't fail. During my free fall, in those terrifying and exhilarating seconds before I released my parachute, Cam's face was burned into the backs of my eyelids. I have to see her one more time.

GUNFIRE PEPPERS the side of the building as I sprint for cover. A few feet ahead of me, Ryker carries Ernesto, who's too weak to stand, let alone run. Muffled pops at regular intervals join the cacophony, and as we duck down behind a shed, I count three dead guerrillas. Damn. Inara didn't lie about her skills.

"Where the fuck is Coop?" Ryker hisses as I load a fresh clip in my pistol, then flatten myself against the wall to fire off a volley of shots towards the observation tower. "I'm going to break his goddamn neck when I find him. He gave away our position."

"If he's not at the rendezvous point, he's probably already

dead." Another burst of enemy fire sends me springing back, and as I hit the shed wall, white hot pain lances through my abdomen.

Without thinking, I roll onto my back and fire two shots up the hill in front of us, taking out the bastard who shot me. Only then does my vision waver. "I'm hit," I manage, but my words sound hollow and raspy.

"Stay with me, Sampson." Ryker yanks a roll of duct tape from his rucksack, pulls up my t-shirt, and curses.

"That...bad?"

After another subtle pop, Inara's voice floats through my comms. "If you boys are going to get out of there, you need to go right the fuck now."

Ryker holds the duct tape in his teeth as he lifts me to my feet. The world tilts. Fire consumes my entire left side, and I let out a roar as the ugly son of a bitch wraps length after length of tape around my torso.

"We leave no one behind," he snaps. With Ernesto tossed over his right shoulder, he lets me lean on his left.

I try to fight him. "You won't make it carrying my ass."

"Then walk. You're a goddamned SEAL, Sampson. If you can't run five hundred yards while bleeding from a stomach wound, you don't deserve to wear the uniform."

"Yessir," I mumble, his words so similar to my former CO's that I can't help but obey.

Inara clears the way for us until we hit the edge of the jungle canopy. With the last of my strength, I squeeze off a round, killing a soldier who springs out of the underbrush. My arm drops, the gun tumbling to the ground. Ryker supports my full weight, maintaining a constant stream of orders to stay conscious, to run, to fight, and I try, but I'm blind, and a dull roar, like the sound of the ocean inside a conch shell, fills my ears.

"Tell...Cam..."

CHAPTER 17

CAM

*O*n the corner of the ceiling, a cluster of glow-in-the-dark stars center me after I wake with a scream in my throat. I almost had them removed when I bought the place, but after a few sleepless nights, I let them stay. Wide awake, mind racing, I reach for my phone. No messages.

When I can't get back to sleep, I tug on a soft tank and shorts and then head for my laptop and coffee. As the rich scent of a Colombian blend fills the room, I log on to VetNet, then promptly forget all about the coffee.

HuskyFan: *Check the logs. Key cards and logins. You almost caught me twice. I can't give up. They'll kill me. But you can stop them.*

"Holy fuck." I rush to reply, hoping he's still online.

FlashPoint: *Do you work at the hotel? How did you know who I was?*

HuskyFan: *I'm a hacker, Camilla. Do you really think finding your name, address, and service record was all that difficult?*

FlashPoint: *Who are you?*

HuskyFan: *Think. You'll figure it out. You helped me through a dark time. I'll never forget you. Goodbye.*

His status changes to offline. A few minutes later, his account disappears completely. I save my chat logs before those vanish as well, then lean back and close my eyes. Whoever HuskyFan is, I think I owe him now.

"WHAT THE HELL?" A single flower—a small daisy—lays across the keyboard in the server room.

"I like daisies. One of the street vendors was selling them this morning." Al had been so surprised when he'd seen me walk in carrying a flower I'd bought on impulse. I told HuskyFan to pick his wife a flower. Could Al be HuskyFan?

Moments after I call up the access logs, Royce slips into the server room. "How are we looking?"

"I don't know." I explain my early morning surprise. "I think… it might be Al. What do you know about him?"

Royce pops two white pills and washes them down with his coffee. "Anti-seizure meds," he says at my raised brow. "Mostly precautionary."

"Mostly? You look like shit, Rolls. Go home. Relax. Or…I don't know…go fishing. Get drunk. Binge watch *House of Cards* or something. Lucas and Orion will be here in an hour. I won't be alone."

"I can't." Royce takes another slow sip of coffee, then sets the cup down next to mine. "Best thing I can do is work. Too much time alone and things get dark pretty quick."

Touching his arm, I try to find the right words to offer comfort, but then my phone buzzes, and I hold my breath. When Lucas's name and number flash across the screen, I try not to let my disappointment show.

Zach and Al called in sick today.

"Bingo."

"Care to explain?" Royce drops down into the chair next to me.

I try not to notice the tremble in his legs as he shifts to get comfortable.

I turn my monitor so he can see the access logs. "Lucas and I were having a drink after the team happy hour on the twentieth." Highlighting two card swipes, I continue. "We left the bar ten minutes after he supposedly entered the server room."

"So, the hacker—Al?—stole his key card. That doesn't explain how he accessed encrypted files."

Waving my hand at the old, now defunct, security camera in the corner of the room, I try to keep the disgust out of my voice. "The strongest password in the world isn't safe from a camera."

"Son of a bitch."

"What do you know about Al? How'd you find him?" Continuing my scan of the logs, I find half a dozen of my own logins at times I was either asleep or engaged in other bed-based activities with West. The pang of loss hits me hard, but I try to ignore the hole in my heart so I can listen to Royce.

"I'd advertised. I wanted to be fully staffed—if not overstaffed —before I had to...leave. His references were excellent, and he'd served with my very first commanding officer."

I tuck a stray curl behind my ear. "He told me he handled radar."

Royce slides over to a free terminal and launches a browser. "Let me pull up his employee file." A few moments later, he snorts. "He lists his army commission as 'Specialist.' Given who he served with? That's bullshit." He picks up his phone. "I still know a few guys I can call for intel."

After he exchanges several off-color jokes and vague updates on his life—no mention of the tumor—with someone he calls "Ace," he asks about Al Hagen. I can't hear what the man on the other end of the line says, but Royce sits up straighter, asks a few quick follow-up questions, then shakes his head. "You're sure?" As he pauses, anger churns in his eyes. "No, that's what I needed. Pretty sure he's involved in some underhanded shit, and the authorities are going to be calling you before long. Thanks a lot. Give my best to Marta."

Defeated, Royce slumps back in his chair. "Well, that's all the evidence I need. Al served four years as a Cyber Operations Analyst. Surveillance and reconnaissance, cyber-attacks, digital forensics, and threat analysis. Sound like skills he put to use breaking into Oversight?"

I can't help my wry laugh. "What the hell do we do now? He's covered his tracks. All we've got are card swipes and logins at times I can prove weren't Lucas or me."

Royce pinches the bridge of his nose. "Keep working on Oversight. Get her up and running. Let me handle the rest. I'm going to have a little heart-to-heart with the rest of the cabling crew. They still on the rooftop deck?"

"Yep."

Pushing to his feet, he looks better than he has in a week. Purpose shines in his gaze, and he rubs his hands together. "This ought to be fun."

"Go get 'em, Lieutenant."

OVERSIGHT LAUNCHES WITHOUT A SINGLE HICCUP, even though Lucas and Royce had to finish installing the last three cameras alone—Royce didn't trust any of the crew Al brought in, and though we don't have any hard evidence, the three men who showed up today are currently downtown talking to the police.

I can't help but take a minute and stare at the software's main interface on the screen in front of me. "We did it, baby. You and me. And Lucas and Orion and Abby and Royce, and even Al, as much as I'd like to kick his ass right now. You're better than you would have been if he'd never touched you."

She throws up her regular system status message—All Clear—and I grin. "Yeah, you are."

Coana's security team waits for me in the employee lounge so I can train them on the new system. The service elevator carries me swiftly to the first floor, where tablet in hand, I check each camera along my route, happy to find the images crisp and clean and perfectly in sync with my movements.

Activating the next camera, I freeze. He's got a hat pulled low over his blond crew cut, but I know that walk, and Al's headed right for me at a fast clip.

My hand spasms as I try to send an alert, and I miss the on-screen button. Al turns the corner, looks up, and stops short.

"Hey, Cam. I…" He shakes his head. "I won't insult you. You're too smart not to have figured it out by now."

"HuskyFan."

With a sigh, he holds out his hand. "Give me the tablet."

"Don't do this." I try to shift my grip so I can send out the alert one-handed, but he snatches the device away.

We're alone in the hall, in an employee-only area, but if I screamed, surely someone in the lounge would hear me. His gaze holds such sadness, though, that I can only take a step back— putting enough distance between us that I can defend myself with my cane if I have to.

"Why?"

"I didn't know you were FlashPoint." Regret softens his tone. "When we started talking, I'd just landed this job. Money was tight, and with losing my vacation pay, I panicked. A couple of my old army buddies knew about this crew out of Seward Park who needed my skills. Ten thousand dollars for what should have been a week's worth of work. I couldn't turn that down."

"Is your wife really pregnant?" My fingers curl tighter around the handle of my cane.

"Yes. Everything I said to you was true." He meets my gaze, and if he's lying, he's the best actor I've ever seen. "You don't understand what's at stake here. They bring in over a hundred thousand dollars a month at each hotel. If I'd tried to leave Emerald City or quit working for them, they would have killed me. They still might. I only came here today so I could prove to them that I tried one more time to reinstall my code. When they find out I failed…"

"Go to the police. Please. Turn yourself in. They'll protect you and your family." I can't help but feel sorry for the man in front of me. Faced with an impossible situation, would I have taken a different path?

Al backs away slowly. "I don't have a choice. By Friday, they'll know I failed. Again." He chokes on his words. At his side, his free hand shakes until he balls it into a fist. "I have to get my family somewhere safe before I take that chance. Keep my secret. Please."

I gesture to the camera pointed directly at us. "I can't. Oversight is live."

Horror widens his eyes, and his entire body tenses. "How long do I have?"

With no hard evidence, the police would only detain him long enough to ensure his employers know he failed. Al twists his wedding ring on his finger. All I can see is his pregnant wife holding their son and crying.

"The cameras don't record audio. By the time I reach a phone—my cell service is really spotty back here—you'd be out of the hotel. Then the police need to show up and take my statement. Forty-five minutes?" Easing myself closer to the wall, I meet his gaze. "You didn't mean to knock me down."

"Forgive me." He rushes towards me, and I hit the wall as he careens past me, managing to only brush my shoulder lightly with his own. Using what West taught me, I control my fall, though the impact still forces a soft yelp from my lips. By the time I'm upright again, he's gone.

CHAPTER 18

CAM

*J*asmine, the sweet scent wafting up from my neighbor's patio, reminds me of my grandmother's perfume, and I'm tipsy enough after three glasses of champagne and a shot of vodka—courtesy of the company party in celebration of our success today—to linger in my memories.

The sting of my father's palm and the salty tang of my tears chase the jasmine away, yet I still find myself trolling my cousin's Facebook page for photos of Mama and Papa. When I find the latest one, the tears I've refused to cry since I joined the army spill onto my cheeks.

Gray won the battle for my mother's hair, and my papa's in a wheelchair next to her. His smile is as bright as ever, but under the blanket spread across his lap, I spy a wasted body. Too many years between us, too many words we can't take back. Yet, I have to try.

Swiping at my damp cheeks, I send a message to my cousin.

Tell Mama and Papa that I love them. Nothing will ever erase the past, and I don't expect forgiveness. I'm asking anyway. I made a stupid mistake—even though I had good intentions. I'm more than my choices

*at seventeen. Going to war, having to survive on my own...I'm a
different person now. I have a good life—a job I love, friends, but I miss
my family.*

Love, Camilla

After another few minutes, I claw my way out of the pool of
self-pity I fell into and launch Netflix. Perhaps *Doctor Who* can
banish my memories back where they belong. Halfway through
The Eleventh Hour, my phone rings. The number's blocked, but I
answer anyway.

Al's voice doesn't carry his usual timbre. "I'm standing outside
of SPD, trying to work up the courage to turn myself in. I told my
wife everything, and she and my son are with an old army buddy
who'll protect them. Why did you let me go?"

I mulled that question over for hours tonight, and after seeing
the photo of my parents, I might have an answer. "Do you
remember the night I told you I'd made a huge mistake and don't
speak to my family anymore?"

"You wouldn't tell me what you did." A siren wails over the
call.

"The details aren't important. But...when I got blown up,
before he bailed on me, Royce called my mama. She hung up on
him. If someone had offered me a chance to repair my relationship
with her that day, to take back what I'd done or find a way to make
things right, I'd have done anything they asked. I understand
desperation, Al. That's why I joined the army in the first place.
Family, too—even though I don't have one anymore."

He's silent for so long, I worry the call's dropped. "Al?"

"My wife hugged me before I left. Told me she loves me." His
voice cracks on the last word.

"Everyone deserves a second chance." Even me, though I'm not
sure I'll get one from my family or from West. "I suspect you're a
good guy at heart, Al. One bad decision doesn't change that. I
hope the police go easy on you. After all, you did the right thing,
in the end."

The call disconnects, and I stare at the darkened screen for several minutes before exhaustion swamps me, and I fall into bed, praying I won't dream.

TEN YEARS out of the army, and I still wake with the sun. After my swim, wrapped in a blanket, the mug of coffee warming my hands, I watch a ferry make its silent trek across the water. In two days, I take over Emerald City Security—at least for the next three months while Royce recovers from his surgery. He told the whole team Friday night, then insisted we all do shots with him to soften the blow. We've only just started to repair things between us, and now...I could lose him. I'm not ready. Not ready to lead either, but he believes in me, as do Lucas and the others.

I had to give a speech after that shot, and I stumbled over a few words, but I told everyone to call me on my shit, then told them we were a team, and we'd get through this together. There were a few tears, mine, Orion's, even Abby's. Mostly, though, we laughed and hugged and toasted Royce.

I limp back into the kitchen, contemplating breakfast, but my doorbell chimes before I pull the eggs from the fridge. This early, I'm expecting the local Girl Scout troop, so when I open the door, I stare directly into a blue t-shirt stretched over a sculpted chest I've dreamed about more than once in the past week.

My gaze travels up, taking in the stubble covering his jaw, the dark circles that bruise his eyes, and the cut on his forehead half-covered by a single butterfly bandage. Though I know I should say something—anything, shock and concern steal my words.

"Can I come in?" Emotion chokes his voice, and when I nod and step back, he moves carefully. His right arm wraps around his torso, and he sets his duffel just inside the door with a small grimace.

The click of the latch reverberates in the silence and shocks me enough to speak. "Are you okay?"

West seems to wrestle with his answer. "Fuck it," he mutters and pulls me tight to his side. "I didn't think I'd ever see you again."

My eyes burn. "I was an ass. When you didn't call, I figured you couldn't forgive me—and I didn't blame you one bit."

"Shh." He nuzzles my hair. "We both made mistakes, angel. I never should have left you that night."

I slide my arms around his waist, and my fingers brush the tell-tale bulge of a thick bandage at the same moment that West's entire body tenses. I draw back, then lift his shirt. A faint reddish tinge mars the white gauze tapped to his abdomen. "Shit. Come sit down."

West drapes his arm over my shoulders as I lead him to the couch, and though he doesn't limp, if I had to guess by the tension in his muscles, he's trying not to lean on me. Once we sit, we stare at one another until I can't stand not touching him for a moment longer, and I brush the backs of my fingers against his cheek. The truth I've tried to ignore since he left slams into me.

I'm falling in love with this man.

He shifts so I can fit myself to his side, and as he rests his cheek against the top of my head, he inhales deeply and a small shudder ripples through him.

"Where the hell did you go after you left me? To take up back alley street fighting?" I want to run my hands over his chest, his arms, his back, checking him for more injuries, but I fear I'll hurt him, so I settle for carefully laying a hand on his thigh.

"Do you know what K&R is?"

"Kidnap and ransom. I had a couple of buddies who talked about getting into that shit after their tours. I don't think they ever did, though. Dangerous work."

"A year before I left the SEALs, we were sent to rescue a high-value target who'd been held hostage for over a year in Hell Mountain. The son of a bitch escaped six hours before we could get to him, but they'd tortured him within an inch of his life, and we found him bleeding out in a cave three clicks away. We spent too long stabilizing him, and the insurgents surrounded us. All the other guys—including Ryker—thought we were done for, but I found a way out. Ryker never forgot that. When he needed a new infiltration specialist for his K&R firm, he came to me. I turned him down not long after we started dating."

"You never mentioned him." I can't keep the hurt from my voice, though I have my own secrets that threaten to tear us apart.

He sighs. "I never thought I'd see him again. But then I couldn't afford the insurance for the kids program. The things I want to do, Cam...I can make a real difference. One job for Ryker —three days, max—covers my expenses for two months." Anguish paints his features, and he tries to pull away, but my small couch leaves him little room. "A small group of guerrillas kidnapped the son of the Colombian president. The kid's only twenty-three. The night we fought...I'd met with Ryker's team and agreed to help them."

"Agreed? You looked like you'd been in a fight." He looks surprised, and my shame skyrockets. "I noticed. But I couldn't see my way past my own issues." Twining our fingers, I meet his gaze. "That's what you were trying to tell me that night."

"The job should have been a cakewalk, but I still didn't want to leave without telling you..." He shakes his head. "Then our communications guy fucked up and let the snipers get a bead on us. Only the second time in my life I've been shot."

He chuckles weakly, but I feel the blood drain from my cheeks. "How bad?"

"Bad enough that Ryker carried my ass out of the jungle, and I ended up unconscious in an illegal Bogota med clinic for two days. I was lucky Ryker and I share the same blood type. Coop didn't live long enough to get out of the compound. As soon as I could walk, Ryker got us on the first transport back to Seattle. We landed less than an hour ago." His fingers are cool as he takes my hands. "Angel, I thought I was going to die. The doc said I came damn close. And all I could think about was how we'd left things."

I don't think I can speak around the lump in my throat, but I cup the back of his neck, leaning forward so our lips are inches apart. "I don't deserve you, West. But so much has happened since that night. Please, forgive me. Tell me you'll give us another chance."

His lips brush mine, and I melt into his embrace, careful of his wounds. His tongue gently teases the seam of my lips, and I part for this man I'm falling in love with, savoring the rasp of his stubble against my cheek, the hard muscles under my palms, and the growing arousal straining his Levi's. I'm half in his lap now, and his fingers tangle in my hair. With a light twist, he urges my head back to meet his gaze.

Eyes the color of the bluest summer sky shimmer slightly with his words. "I love you, Cam. I passed out begging Ryker to find you and tell you, afraid I wouldn't wake up again. But…love requires trust, and trust works both ways."

"I know." Still reeling from knowing how close I came to losing him, I rest my head on his chest, letting the steady beat of his heart calm me. "When I got blown up, Royce blamed himself. He put out the fire eating through my suit, got a tourniquet around my leg, and held my hand as I screamed for what felt like hours waiting for the MediVac to show. And then he disappeared."

A single tear soaks into the soft blue cotton. My life story unfolds as West holds me close.

"When I was fifteen, my father lost his job, and my grand-mother came to live with us. We didn't have any money, but I was smart, and the honors program at my high school gave me a computer. Part of a fund to get more minority girls interested in science, computers, and math. They signed me up for a college-level programming class, and to meet with my professor, I needed a webcam."

I wipe my hands on my thighs, unprepared for the nerves that seem certain to send me over the edge. "I told my parents I was doing medical transcription at night to help pay the bills. But really, I put on a bikini and danced for men." A laugh escapes, too high and thin to be anything other than hysterical. "After the first six months, I'd saved enough to pay for almost anything I wanted. Including a collapsible pole I hid under my bed."

I risk a glance at West. If he's horrified, I can't tell, so I rush to tell him the rest. "By seventeen, I had a full college fund my parents didn't know about. But a month before graduation, Nana broke her hip. I couldn't hear my mother knocking on the door, so she had my father break the lock. The look on his face... The day after I graduated, Papa told me I had a month to move out. I'd brought too much shame to the family to stay."

West balls his hands into fists. "You were seventeen."

"I was an adult in his eyes. If I could do adult things, I could support myself. I'd been accepted to Stanford, but college didn't mean a thing without my family. Papa always said how honorable it was to serve your country. So I asked for a deferral on my admission, and I enlisted on my eighteenth birthday. Two days before his deadline."

He swears when I tell him my mother wouldn't even speak to me when I thought I was going to lose my leg, rubs my back when I talk about Lucas, and tightens his embrace when I recall the day Royce told me about his tumor.

"My life has been one big broken promise, West. I learned early on to guard my heart, to trust no one, and then I met you." Angling my head so he can see the truth in my eyes, I take a deep breath. "No one has ever understood me like you do. I'm sorry I couldn't see that until now."

I straddle him, careful to avoid the bullet wound, and cup his cheeks. "I spent every night we were apart wishing I could talk to you, wishing I *had* talked to you. I won't make that mistake again."

I seal my words with a tender kiss, and when our lips part, he brushes a lock of hair away from my cheek. "I won't let you. You're it for me, angel. My life never flashed before my eyes when I was bleeding out in the jungle. I only saw you. I lived for you."

My heart skips a beat as I stare at this man I don't ever want to be without. "I love you, West. That's a promise."

CHAPTER 19

*H*er soft breath tickles my cheek. The sheet does little to hide the gentle swell of her breasts, the curve of her hip. We covered two lifetimes of secrets in a single day, fueled by pizza, beer, and painkillers. Now, the light of the moon casts my angel's face in a pale glow, and I've never felt so content.

The doc in Bogota warned me against getting on the plane, but once I'd regained consciousness and realized I'd been out for two days, nothing could keep me down.

Cam whimpers in her sleep. The bandage sticks to my skin as I stroke my hand down her arm. "I'm here, angel. You're safe."

I watch her until I'm sure she's settled, then stifle my groan as I swing my legs over the side of the bed. This is going to hurt. Standing leads to a wave of dizziness, but I breathe through the pain and stumble out to Cam's living room to retrieve my duffel.

With fresh bandages in my hand, I make my way to the bathroom, and once I'm shut inside, I peel off the bloody gauze.

Better than I'd feared. Only one stitch threatens to pop, and while the wound oozes, the antibiotics the doc forced on me seem to be working.

"Let me help." Cam slips into the bathroom, her gaze locked on mine. "You should have listened to your doctor."

"Pretty sure he was a veterinarian."

Her mouth forms a sexy little "o" as she eases the bandage from my hands. "And you're going out on one of these missions again?"

"Ryker spent fourteen months in the hands of some of the worst men in the world. Now, he wants to save others from the same fate. I can help him. I...don't know what I'll do the next time he calls, but I won't make that decision without you."

With a gentle touch, she presses the fresh bandage to my side, and her naked breasts brush my arm. My cock stirs, reminding me just how long I've waited to taste her.

"Easy there, West. You're in no condition for extracurricular activities." Cam grins at me in the mirror, but when I stroke my hand down her flat stomach to the curls that cover her mound, she shivers.

Her arousal coats my fingers as I continue my slow exploration, dipping inside her once, twice. As I stroke her clit, her knees buckle, and I brace her against the counter so I can scrape my teeth over one peaked nipple.

"Fuck, Cam. I dreamed of this when I was barely able to remember my own name in that filthy shack on the edge of Bogota." Dropping to my knees, I worship the tiny bud at the apex of her thighs, leaving her panting and desperate by the time I pull away. "Bed. Now."

"Uh huh. You'll...pay for this...later."

I probably will. Do I care? Hell no. The sight of her toned ass is all I need to invigorate me and make me forget the pain as I follow her, and we collapse on the bed together.

She stops me when I kneel between her thighs. "Inside me. Now."

Those lifetimes of secrets we shared? She's on the pill, and we're both clean, so I don't hesitate, nudging her entrance with the head of my cock. As she angles her hips, I slide home, and her inner walls grip me so hard, I have to grit my teeth so I don't lose control.

"You're so fucking perfect, Cam."

In the soft light, her eyes shine. "Make me come, West. Make me yours."

"Oh, you're mine, angel." I thrust hard, and she whimpers in pleasure. As I work my hips, she rakes her nails down my back. "I love you," I manage as my balls tighten and the world starts to shimmer around us.

"West!" She implodes as I reach down and massage her clit, and I lose control so I can tumble over the edge with her.

I'm not sure I can move, lying face down, my head buried in her pillow. Cam snuggles against my side. As I drift off to sleep, sated, warm, and content, I hear her whisper, "I love you, too."

HELLO,

Thank you for reading *Breaking His Code*. This book was truly a labor of love for me. One I wasn't sure would ever see the light of day.

I started this book two full years before I published it, and in the middle of writing, my entire world turned upside down. Everything stopped. For a while, I wondered if I'd ever write again.

But I came through that dark time stronger. The things that happened—well, they're not important—except that they made me who I am today. I happen to like that person.

There's a lot of me in Cam. More than I ever realized until the story was done.

The men and women from the *Away From Keyboard* series are what I like to call **beautifully broken**.

They all have scars. They're all damaged in various ways.

Whether physically or emotionally, they've all been broken in the past. But their flaws and their scars and how they deal with them? That's what makes them beautiful. Perfect. **REAL**.

There are at least ten books planned for the *Away From Keyboard* series. Each book can be read as a standalone, but past characters will make appearances now and again, so you'll never have to truly say goodbye.

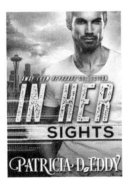

I HOPE you'll check out Royce and Inara's story, *In Her Sights*. I know Royce wasn't the nicest character in *Breaking His Code*, but now that he and Cam are rebuilding their friendship...well...he goes through some intense changes.

And Inara? I have two words for you. Female Sharpshooter.

One-click IN HER SIGHTS now!

YOU CAN ALSO JOIN my Facebook group, **Patricia's Unstoppable Forces**, for sneak peeks of future books, character drive-bys, and the chance to help shape my future novels!

Love, Patricia

P.S. Reviews are like candy for authors.

Did you know that reviews are like chocolate (or cookies or cake) for authors?

Honest reviews of my books help bring them to the attention of other readers.

If you've enjoyed this book, I'd be eternally grateful if you could spend just five minutes leaving a review (it can be as short as you like) on the book's retail page. Just click here.

ALSO BY PATRICIA D. EDDY

AWAY FROM KEYBOARD

Dive into a steamy mix of geekery and military might with the men and women of Emerald City Security and North-West Protective Services.

Breaking His Code

In Her Sights

On His Six

Second Sight

By Lethal Force

Fighting For Valor

Call Sign: Redemption

MIDNIGHT COVEN

These novellas will take you into the darker side of the paranormal with vampires, witches, and more.

Forever Kept

Immortal Hunter

Wicked Omens

ELEMENTAL SHIFTER

Hot werewolves and strong, powerful elementals. What's not to love?

A Shift in the Water

A Shift in the Air

BY THE FATES

Check out the By the Fates series if you love dark and steamy tales of
witches, devils, and an epic battle between good and evil.

By the Fates, Freed

Destined: A By the Fates Story

By the Fates, Fought

By the Fates, Fulfilled

IN BLOOD

If you love hot Italian vampires and and a human who can hold her own
against beings far stronger, then the In Blood series is for you.

Secrets in Blood

Revelations in Blood

HOLIDAYS AND HEROES

Beauty isn't only skin deep and not all scars heal. Come swoon over sexy
vets and the men and women who love them.

Mistletoe and Mochas

Love and Libations

RESTRAINED

Do you like to be tied up? Or read about characters who do? Enjoy a fresh BDSM series that will leave you begging for more.

In His Silks

Christmas Silks

All Tied Up For New Year's

In His Collar

ABOUT THE AUTHOR

Patricia D. Eddy lives in many worlds. Witches, vampires, and shifters inhabit one of them, military men and women fill another, with sexy Doms and strong subs carving out the final slice of her literary universe. She admits to eighteen novels (though there are at least five unfinished drafts on her desk right now), all while working a full-time job, running half-marathons, and catering to the every whim of her three cats. Despite this whirlwind, she still finds time to binge watch *Doctor Who,* all of the Netflix Marvel shows, and most recently, *The Handmaid's Tale.* Oh, and she hopes to one day be able to say that she plays the guitar. Right now, she mostly tortures the strings until they make noise.

You can reach Patricia all over the web...
patriciadeddy.com
patricia@patriciadeddy.com

f facebook.com/patriciadeddyauthor

🐦 twitter.com/patriciadeddy

📷 instagram.com/patriciadeddy

BB bookbub.com/profile/patricia-d-eddy

Made in the USA
Coppell, TX
09 June 2022

78667246R00105